MAUVE DESERT

MAUVE DESERT

a novel

Nicole Brossard

translated by
Susanne de Lotbinière-Harwood

Coach House Press · Toronto

Originally published in 1987 as *Le Désert mauve*
by Éditions de l'Hexagone, Montréal, Québec.

Copyright © 1987 Éditions de l'Hexagone and Nicole Brossard
Translation Copyright © 1990 Susanne de Lotbinière-Harwood

Words and phrases in English and italics in the original
French edition of the novel are in English and roman type
in this translation. – S.L.H. & N.B.

The punctuation of this novel adheres carefully to
the author's and translator's instructions.

Published with the assistance of the Canada Council
and the Ontario Arts Council.

CANADIAN CATALOGUING IN PUBLICATION

Brossard, Nicole. 1943- .
[Désert mauve. English]
Mauve desert

Translation of: Le désert mauve.
ISBN 0-88910-389-5

I. Title. II. Title: Désert mauve. English

PS8503.R62D4713 1990   C843'.54   C90-095280-6
PQ3919.2.B76D4713 1990

Reading is going toward something that is about to be, and no one yet knows what it will be....

ITALO CALVINO

CONTENTS

MAUVE DESERT

Laure Angstelle

𝓐

ARROYO PRESS

The desert is indescribable. Reality rushes into it, rapid light. The gaze melts. Yet this morning. Very young, I was already crying over humanity. With every new year I could see it dissolving in hope and in violence. Very young, I would take my mother's Meteor and drive into the desert. There I spent entire days, nights, dawns. Driving fast and then slowly, spinning out the light in its mauve and small lines which like veins mapped a great tree of life in my eyes.

I was wide awake in the questioning but inside me was a desire which free of obstacles frightened me like a certitude. Then would come the pink, the rust and the grey among the stones, the mauve and the light of dawn. In the distance, the flashing wings of a tourist helicopter.

Very young I had no future like the shack on the corner which one day was set on fire by some guys who 'came from far away,' said my mother who had served them drinks. Only one of them was armed, she had sworn to me. Only one among them. All the others were blond. My mother always talked about men as if they had seen the day in a book. She would say no more and go back to her television set. I could see her profile and the reflection of the little silver comb she always wore in her hair and to which I attributed magical powers. Her apron was yellow with little flowers. I never saw her wearing a dress.

I was moving forward in life, wild-eyed with arrogance. I was fifteen. This was a delight like the power of dying or of driving into the night with circles under my eyes, absolutely delirious spaces edging the gaze.

I was well-acquainted with the desert and the roads running through it. Lorna, this friend of my mother's, had introduced me to erosion, to all the ghosts living in the stone and the dust. She had described landscapes, some familiar, some absolutely incompatible with the vegetation and barren soil of my childhood. Lorna was inventing. I knew she was because even I knew how to distinguish between a Western diamondback and a rattlesnake, between a troglodyte and a mourning turtledove. Lorna was inventing. Sometimes she seemed to be barking, so rough and unthinkable were her words. Lorna had not known childhood, only young girls after school whom she would ostentatiously arrange to meet at noon. The girls loved kissing her on the mouth. She loved girls who let themselves be kissed on the mouth.

The first time I saw Lorna I found her beautiful and said the word 'bitch.' I was five years old. At supper my mother was smiling at her. They would look at each other and when they spoke their voices were full of intonations. I obstinately observed their mouths. Whenever they pronounced words starting with *m*, their lips would disappear for a moment then, swollen, reanimate with incredible speed. Lorna said she liked moly and salmon mousse. I spilled my glass of milk and the tablecloth changed into America with Florida seeping under the salt-shaker. My mother mopped up America. My mother always pretended not to notice when things were dirtied.

I often took to the road. Long before I got my driver's license. At high noon, at dusk, even at night, I would leave with my mother yelling sharp words at me which would get lost in the parking lot dust. I always headed for the desert because very young I wanted to know why in books they forget to mention the desert. I knew my mother would be alone like a woman can be but I was fleeing the magical reflection of the comb in her hair, seeking the burning reflections of the blinding sun, seeking the night in the dazzled eyes of hares, a ray of life. 'Let me confront aridity,' and I would floor the accelerator, wild with the damned energy of my fifteen years. Some day I would reach the right age and time as necessary as a birth date to get life over with. Some day I would be fast so fast, sharp so sharp, some day, faced with the necessity of dawn, I would have forgotten the civilization of men who came to the desert to watch their equations explode like a humanity. I was driving fast, alone like a character cut out of history. Saying 'so many times I have sunk into the future.'

At night there was the desert, the shining eyes of antelope jack rabbits, *senita* flowers that bloom only in the night. Lying under the Meteor's headlights was the body of a humanity that did not know Arizona. Humanity was fragile because it did not suspect Arizona's existence. So fragile. I was fifteen and hungered for everything to be as in my body's fragility, that impatient tolerance making the body necessary. I was an expert driver, wild-eyed in mid-night, capable of going forward in the dark. I knew all that like a despair capable of setting me free of everything. Eternity was a shadow cast in music, a fever of the brain making it topple over into the tracings of highways. Humanity was fragile, a gigantic hope suspended over cities. Everything was fragile, I knew it, I had always known it. At fifteen I pretended I had forgotten mediocrity. Like my mother, I pretended that nothing was dirtied.

Shadows on the road devour hope. There are no shadows at night, at noon, there is only certitude traversing reality. But reality is a little trap, little shadow grave welcoming desire. Reality is a little passion fire that pretexts. I was fifteen and with every ounce of my strength I was leaning into my thoughts to make them slant reality toward the light.

And now to park the car in front of the Red Arrow Motel. Heat, the Bar. The bar's entire surface resembles a television image: elbows everywhere leaning like shadows and humanity's trash repeating themselves. I have a beer and nobody notices I exist.

CHAPTER ONE

Longman puts his briefcase on the bed. He has been hot, he loosens his tie. He heads for the bathroom. He thinks about the explosion, he thinks about it and it's not enough. Something. He knows some lovely little footpaths, delicately shaded areas. He hesitates in front of the mirror. He washes his hands. He thinks about the explosion, he thinks about it and nothing happens in his head. He removes his jacket, throws it on the bed. A ballpoint pen falls to the floor. He does not bend down. He lights a cigarette. He fingers the brim of his felt hat which he almost never takes off. He thinks about the explosion. For the pleasure of sounds he recites a few sentences in Sanskrit, the same ones which earlier delighted his colleagues. He paces the floor. His cigarette smoke follows him about like a spectral presence. Longman knows the magic value of formulas. He thinks about the explosion. The slightest error could have disastrous consequences. Longman stretches out with white visions then orange ones then the ground beneath his feet turns to jade – I / am / become / Death – now we are all sons of bitches. Longman rests his head on the equation.

I had the power over my mother to take her car from her at the most unexpected moment. My mother had the unsuspected power to arouse in me a terrible solitude which, when I saw her in such closeness to Lorna, devastated me for then there was between them just enough silence for the thought of their commingled flesh to infiltrate me. One night unexpectedly in the obscurity of their room I came upon my mother, her shoulders and the nape of her neck braced like an existence toward Lorna's nakedness.

I'm driving. Howling, rock-jaw'd, mouth full of lyrics I sing to the same beat as the woman's voice exploding the radio. A voice of doom interrupts the song. I howl. I lean on the announcer interrupting the music until the earthquake ebbs into the distance, tidal wave, resorbs into the Pacific blue. The desert is civilization. I don't like leaving my mother at night. I fear for her. Mothers are as fragile as civilization. They must not be forgotten in front of their television sets. Mothers are spaces. I love driving fast in my mother's Meteor. I love the road, the vanishing horizon, feeling dawn's fresh emptiness. I never panic in the desert. In the middle of the night or even in the midst of a sandstorm as the windshield slowly covers up, I know how to be isolated from everything, concrete and unreal like a character confined to the steering wheel of an old Meteor. In the dark of the dust I know how to exist. I listen to the dreadful sound, the roar of wind and sand against the car's metal body. I yield totally to blindness. I lightly press two fingers against each eyelid and look inside the intimate *species*, at time going by in the back of my mind. I see seconds, small silvery scars, moving along like creatures. I recognize the trace of creatures who have passed through there where seconds form pyramids, spirals, among the remains, beautiful sandstone chevrons. Only once words I was unable to read. And their form soon faded as if it were a partial transcription of light deep in the mind.

I was driving avidly. Choosing the night the desert to thus expose myself to the violence of the moment which propels consciousness. I was fifteen and before me space, space far off tapering me down like a civilization in reverse, city lost in the trembling air. In my mother's Meteor I was exemplary solitude with, at the tip of my toes, a brake to avoid all disasters and to remind me of the insignificance of despair amid snakes and cacti in the bluest night of all ravings.

I am my mother's laughter when I pale in the face of humanity's distress. Never did my mother cry. I never saw her cry. My mother was unable to imagine that solitude could be like an exactness of being. She trembled when faced with humanity's noises but no solitude really reached her. In the worst moments of her existence my mother would conclude: 'This is a man, we need a bed; this is a woman, we need a room.' My mother was as obstinate as a man struggling with the desert. She did not like men but she defended the desert like a feeling leaguing her with men. She was a woman without expression and this frightened me.

Every time I think of my mother I see girls in swimsuits lying by the Motel pool. This motel, purchased in 1950, my mother renovated it and spent fifteen years paying it off with polite gestures, discipline and energy repeated in the heat of Tucson afternoons. But before Lorna's arrival, everything is vague. Vague and noisy like the to-and-fro of travelers, of suppliers, of the chambermaid.

Lorna's presence will always be linked in my memory with my first years of school and especially with learning to read and write. I liked to read but don't remember reading otherwise than in Lorna's presence. She would watch me, static watcher, monitoring every blink of my eyelids, spying any flutter of sensation, the slightest sign upon my face liable to betray an emotion. I would follow her little game with a discrete eye but when I happened to look up, it was my turn to follow upon her lips the strange alphabet which seemed to constitute a dream in her gaze. I would then invariably ask the question: 'What are we eating?' as if this could keep her at bay or protect the intimate nature of what I had experienced while reading.

One day when looking for some blank paper to draw on I saw, at the far end of the kitchen, Lorna and my mother sitting on the same chair. My mother was on Lorna's lap, who was holding her by the waist with her right arm. With her left hand Lorna was scribbling. Their legs were all entwined and my mother's apron was folded over Lorna's thigh. I asked Lorna what she was writing. She hesitated then spun out some sentence to the effect that she was unable to read the marks her hand had drawn. I was about to exclaim, to say that ... it made no sense when I noticed the ease of Lorna's hand in my mother's hair.

Yet that night. Very young I learned to love the fire from the sky, torrential lightning branched out over the city like thinking flowing in the mind. On dry storm nights I would become tremors, detonations, total discharge. Then surrender to all the illuminations, those fissures which like so many wounds lined my virtual body, linking me to the vastness. And so the body melts like a glimmer of light in the abstract of words. Eyes, existence give in before that which comes forth inside us, certitude. The desert drinks everything in. Furor, solitude.

In the desert there is the pursuit of breaks clouds sometimes make. Sometimes they are like little lead pellets the sun shoots toward the horizon to signify tomorrow's coming future. I am well acquainted with lead, copper, cartridges and all weapons. I know weapons. Any desert girl learns at a very young age how to hold a weapon and to drive a car. Any young girl learns that what glitters under the sun can also hurt or excite feeling so utterly that shadow itself turns to crimson.

CHAPTER TWO

Longman is not asleep. He is thinking about the explosion. He has stretched out fully dressed. His shoes are dusty. He is thinking about art, the art of the energy spectrum. He gets up and walks to the dresser. In the second drawer the small magazine in flesh and purplish tones lies in its place under the white, orange and jade colored folders. He takes the magazine, lies down again after rearranging the pillow. He turns the pages, watching and waiting for something to happen. 'Now we are all sons of bitches.' The explosion will occur. In the silence of the room the man eyes the genitals, their coloration. He does not see the faces. The faces, shadow of shadows, make white circles around the genitals. Then the circles make a noise like an explosion. He shuts his eyes. Dust falls slowly like that winter at Princeton, the eve of his twentieth birthday. Longman is unable to sleep. Neither can his neighbors in the next room. To the right he hears him pacing, to the left he hears him shuffling his math sheets. Longman knows *beautiful* blue lakes, the *great* petrified forest with its amethyst trees everlasting. He dreams of a past. It is snowing in the everlasting. The spectres are splendors. Now that earth and death and tongue became thy shall not. Longman hears the noise of the explosion. Heart leaps, body leaps. A final shiver. He strokes his felt hat. He lights a cigarette.

Here in the desert, fear is precise. Never an obstacle. Fear is real, is nothing like anguish. It is as necessary as a day of work well done. It is localized, familiar and inspires no fantasies. Here there are only wind, thorns, snakes, wolf-spiders, beasts, skeletons: the soil's very nature.

At the Motel though, fear is diffuse, televised like a rape, a murder, a fit of insanity. It torments the mind's gullible side, obstructs dreams, bruises the soul's trouble.

I was fifteen and I'm talking about fear, for fear, one thinks about it only after the fact. Precise fear is beautiful. Perhaps it is possible after all to fantasize fear like a blind spot producing a craving for eternity, like a hollow imaginary moment leaving in the pit of the stomach a powerful sensation, a renewed effect of ardor.

I remember that when Lorna arrived my mother often spoke of fear. A livid fear, she said, a slow fear. Lorna seemed to like this fear. When talking, when laughing, when walking, in everything, Lorna fanned my mother's fear, a fear that made her restless and transformed her voice. Whenever Lorna launched her muscled body into the pool, my mother would cry out: 'Lor, please' but Lorna only dripped all the more wetly, enjoying my mother's uneasy fear with her eyes. Then her arms would sweep me away with her and my mother once again, my mother would lean over the water, her face worried. I could see the shape of her body. The shape of her head was above the water like a comet. My mother was a giant and then I would surface.

Some day perhaps I will tell my life story. Some day when I am no longer fifteen with a heart whose spirit has a sense of wonder. It's saying it all when I talk about the night and the desert for in so doing I am stepping through the immediate legend of my life on the horizon. I have abused the stars and the screens of life, I have opened up roads of sand, I have quenched my thirst and my instinct like so many words in view of the magical horizon, alone, maneuvering insanely so as to respond to the energy traversing me like a necessity, an avalanche of being. I was fifteen and I knew how to designate people and objects. I knew that a hint of threat meant only kilometers more to go in the night. I pressed on the accelerator and clash, sweat, fear, oh how fragile the body when it's so hot, so dark, so pale, immense silence.

Night! Yes, I have seen dawn. Often. But at night, dawn was already beaming spectral in the spectacle of swirling sand. I was driving. I was howling in life, at night on the highway. By day it was the pool, girls in swimsuits and my mother at the end of the line busy with Motel business or in front of the television set, busy with fear. Lorna would approach her and my mother would let herself be cherished and my mother would choose her. It was daily and true, informal between them except that my gaze would come and suspend their gestures thus compelling their bodies to strange rituals to compensate for the lost equilibrium or the ripening trajectory of loving arms.

Some nights the dryness was dark and it fascinated me to think that dark, dryness was a word just as I myself was a girl like a word in life. But I could exist without comparison. This was certain, as certain as the thirst to come when precautions are not taken before heading out and lips wrinkle, crack in the strong dry wind.

I was always certain of everything. Of faces, of the time, of the sky, of distances, of the horizon. I was certain of everything except words. The fear of words. Slow fear. Strains to say. Strains to hear. Pain in all my veins.

At the end of a May afternoon, when I had veered off the road to get a closer look at an old *saguaro*'s half-wounded, half-agonized silhouette, and was singing as usual – fever, fever, forever going away –, I felt fear heavy to bear. The *saguaro* swayed, real and unreal. The *saguaro*, words, all my reflexes were in slow motion and soon there was no more day, no more dawn, no more road, no more cactus, barely the instinct to think that words are nonetheless but words.

In the glove compartment, under the revolver, was a little notebook I used for keeping a record of oil changes and other details concerning the car's maintenance. A pencil from the Helljoy Garage, makeshift paperclip, held the unglued pages together. So I wrote about that, I wrote *that and that again and more, that excited me, grabbed me like you can't believe to write all that with explosions in my head, little chalky trails through the canyons. I know the parchment-like epidermis of the great agonizing cacti, all of it, the burrowing animal leaving its trace.* Fear goes away, fear slopes away.

The horizon is curving. Around the great *saguaro,* the trembling atmosphere. On my way back to the Motel I run the last light filled with the desire of my mother's face and Lorna's. My mother is absent. Lorna is watching a television show. Crazy gleam of light in my room and my fingers there, that's it, there, yet sways, amuses me, *aways* me.

That same night the awareness of words circuited my feeling, wrapped round it, got it turning in the wrong sense. My impression was of a thousand detours, of grave gestures within matter. The sensation of living, the sensation of dying, writing as an alternative among images. Then reality became an IMAGE. I fell asleep at dawn, strapped in my sheets, *object* of the image.

I now know delayed-action fear. I spend hours in front of the television set. I think and come close to all that like a child skirts silence and the muffled noise of voices transmitting anxiety. I know reality. I know humanity so suddenly like a shadow in my eyes. It moves slowly, so slowly, humanity, in its desires, slow snake in the desert, it hides, it sheds. It moves no more, is nothing but deserted skin. But the skin is there, similar, hollow, just like life at the foot of *senitas* and *ocotillos.* Fear of the hollow skin is 'devilish' like a little fetish reality on beautiful orange and jade footpaths. Skin frightens tourists. That's skin.

That same month my mother was sad and Lorna like my mother. I harassed my mother to make her read the *little* I had written. My mistakes! I wanted her to correct it all. I would leave the composition book on the television set or on the floor, in plain view. At night I could hear her telling Lorna stories she had read in *Time* or in *Convention Globe*. At the end of the story someone would die, leave or reveal a secret. So I would turn up the television and devote body and soul to the overpowerful fear of reality.

Ever since I had written in the maintenance notebook I could truly see reality close up. Customers came from Texas, from Wisconsin, from Minnesota. A lot of old people. A few travelling salesmen, once or twice some women together for whom existing seemed really well-founded. I sometimes eavesdropped on conversations at the bar. Customers talked about sports or money. Some supported their statements with numbers, others pounced on a word to turn it into a juicy sentence and provoke laughter. Shoulders shook, you offered your neighbor a cigarette, you toasted. Then boredom, broads and business all over again.

One evening I was finally able to see this Angela Parkins my mother often talked about. She must have been forty years old. She was a geometrist and came here every first Tuesday of the month. She sat at the bar and always talked with two men whom my mother said were engineers. That evening I sat at the bar hoping to overhear a conversation that would unravel the mystery my mother had created around Angela Parkins. But the detailed discussion concerned structure and perspective in words mostly unknown to me. Then Angela Parkins turned to my mother and chatted with her a bit, now using simple words that resonated inside me, tasty and colorful like some intimate thing.

The evening went on as usual until Angela Parkins raised her voice, hysterical, bordering on intoxication. Her voice got carried away, tumbled into the smoky space. Angela Parkins left the Bar before eleven and I retired at about the same time. Reality had a meaning, but which one?

The next day I informed my mother of my departure for New Mexico. I had telephoned Grazie, a cousin living in Albuquerque, and she had invited me to spend a few days.

CHAPTER THREE

The man's eyes were wild and arrogant. He was raising his head then lowering it and every time, the explosion in his head. There was the floor, the ceiling, the walls and the explosion. Everything was on fast forward in his body subjected to his thoughts. He was lost. The dust was there, cold reason falling out on his shoulders. He would never recover from winter, he who so loved little footpaths and dew smells. The walls of the room were, against all logic, full of his shadow. He tried concentrating on a Sanskrit poem. Too late. Already the ashes, already the blood, already the cries, tremendous mouths, stilled in the night's silence, glistened like crystals in his every neuron. So longman started drawing figures on the walls full of his shadow. Then his exhausted body slid down the wall. The long shadow fainted. The explosion was perfect in jade.

I was driving slowly. It was broad daylight, hot and sweat. Total insanity to be driving like this in the high noon sun. An exhausting solitude I inflicted upon myself as if to recapture that time from before writing, before reality. I was driving and the desert was now real, dangerous, full of daggers, blades and venom. I had sworn not to drink anything during the first five hours. I wanted heat and thirst whole, excessive. I wanted my body feverish, to lose nothing of its fluency, of its exuberance. I wanted it both in focus and out of the frame, overlayed on the hyperreality of blue, compelled in its every cell to acquire a taste along the reality of roads for all the ephemeral shapes crossing my gaze. I wanted no part of myth. Only what's body, sweat, thirst.

I sum up reality in the slowness of kilometers. I sum up my life in the blinding light. One day between Phoenix and the petrified forest, I had a dream, as flamboyant as a rapture, a drift in space *the throat has crazy cracks horizons horrible zones of laughter, cascades that ransack the ages and the cages of eyes bewildered in the impossible beauty of the lapses and torments that burden thinking.*

I had now entered the fear of the unspeakable, in the frenzy of words involuntarily I was abdicating to silence. In the desert one gives in without ulterior motive with the pliancy of a being surrendered to space. The horizon is a mirage that orients the thirsting body.

I was driving, restless thinking, heading toward Albuquerque and Grazie. To Grazie I would talk about Angela Parkins, I would talk to her about a woman met in the night of a Tuesday. I would shiver, I would stammer. I would talk about Angela Parkins like about a dream in the petrified forest. Grazie would understand, she would say: 'Talk, go ahead and talk. Tell me all about it. Talk to me about Angela Parkins, about all her secrets yapped out in the Motel Bar. Talk to me about the women and about Angela, their gestures, their devastating laughter, their eyes and their smiles meeting, about fear that alarms thoughts. Talk to me, volatile and flushed, be snake and slowness with beauty, be fire and rigor. Light me so that the desert may sink deep into us and the ultrasounds of our childhood be reborn. Light me because I might some day.'

Grazie was two months older than I. We were 'distant sisters,' meaning girls whose mothers had named them thus one evening when both pregnant they had seduced each other and shared something like a twenty-four hour hope. We were daughters hoped-for in the night of our mothers being lovers. I know reality. My mother had talked to me about a trip to Dante's View, had told me about a walk taken and a vantagepoint, the most striking one at Dante's View, the most gorgeous at Badwater and at Artist Drive. Then she had added: 'Mélanie, nonetheless night.'

I'm driving slowly toward plain certitude. Grazie is expecting me in Albuquerque. At the junction of ⑩ and ㉕ are dozens of motorcycles, guys smoking as they look at the sky. Two girls are talking. One of them flashes me a peace and love sign while the other one, barely set back in the spatial plane, gives me a violent fuck with her finger, then with her fist. I press on the accelerator. I know reality. Fear, it doesn't matter when you accelerate; fear vanishes like a dark spot in the rearview mirror.

The road was a time warp lost in the horizon's trembling air. I was fifteen and ahead of me reality to help me bypass existence. And then there was freedom! Where I grew up freedom is worn heart-side like a weapon. It can just as well serve to overcome fear and nostalgia as to make noise inside of kidneys, jaws and vaginas. Where I grew up women would put freedom on their cheeks: it smelled like incense, sleek skin, medicinal, while the men got off a good shot of freedom at everything that moved.

I lost the desert. I lost the desert in the night of writing. There is always a first time, a first night that blurs passions, that confuses our sense of direction. A first time when it must be acknowledged that words can reduce reality to its smallest unit: *matter* of fact. Now *matter* of fact must bring the desert back to life and color be returned to troglodytes, to coral snakes, to rufous bobcats. The antelope jack rabbit must once again be able to quick-change the color of its flanks from tan to white, and the mysterious stones walking Death Valley to leave traces of their passage in the clay. *Matter* of fact must return like a desire of the desert so that once again images can help me create a vacuum as though they were tiny little suction cups lodged in my mind.

There are memories for digging into words without defiling graves. I cannot get close to any you. There is no otherness, only alternation in appearance. I need flexibility and tension. Albuquerque must not explode in my head.

Why do I think words like this, why upon entering Albuquerque a fit of laughter, the fatigue of a fit of laughter, fever upon entering reality's sudden beauty of a game?

Grazie proved tender a companion. She was completely captivated, both mocking and curious, by the tattoo on my left shoulder, traced its outline with her soft fingers, said that some day she would get a unicorn on one of her buttocks. Then we made sand witches like when we were children and I drank two liters of water. 'Are you alright? Yes, there's a dance tomorrow. My dress and look, you'll see, it's wonderful.' There are sentences between us. Who said that? 'I'm tired, tomorrow. Then we'll go there. It's great. It was beautiful. I hurt my index finger. It's like falling into a trap or into a blue word. I put a photograph near the big mirror. It's such a likeness. In the half-light a piece of wood reminded me. Oh yes! What for? We're fine here, together.'

I'm thinking of Lorna who never takes the time to breathe between sentences. Lorna is intelligible only in my mother's arms.

'Make room for me in the bed. Move over. OK, I'm turning the light on to read all night. Grazie, you know our mothers were once lovers. Now it's time to go to sleep. If you want to stay up, I you I no I yes so sleep otherwise ... What! Yes, it's soft. You're taking up the whole pillow. This is my side. Grazie ... just this once, it's so soft.'

Life is like a sensation on remote location. Tonight I will lie next to Grazie's desert and her incense-filled sleep.

CHAPTER FOUR

Somewhere in the night of his black-out, longman recovered his senses. It was night's silence. No body was moving, neither in the room on the left, nor on the right. Longman got up with difficulty as if he had been drinking all night. He leaned against the wall then leaned over and picked up his hat which lay on the floor. After all, he thought, *tomorrow* the sky will be blue. But daybreak lay shattered all over in his mind. On the walls, figures oozed and merged with the words that followed him, that followed him all around the little room. Longman who had invented the explosion like a hope for beauty knew he would be unable to survive the beauty of the equations. He would not survive his image. Longman felt fragile, full of a bitter solitude. He saw himself broken, mirror, fraction, incapable of figuring out his wound. So he sank impotent into prayer. Eyelids closed, hands joined, he pleaded for a long time, insensitive to the debris falling out on his shoulders.

This morning Grazie and her mother have gone out to run some errands. Here I am, motionless in the room, watching what is going on in the street. Nothing. Only reality. Oh to take my leave! Some day I will exit reality, the scandal of it. Beauty is before reality.

Today I will take the desert road again and get back to my mother and Lorna as well as the murmur of girls in swimsuits by the side of the pool. Reality will be real like a G-string in the jukebox glow of lights, like a hired killer looking at his instructions manual. The mind is fragile, it takes many superstitions to win it over without damaging anything around it. There is no more desert. Grazie will never be fifteen.

On the way back I drove fast, fast so fast. Why linger while imagining kisses, embraces, while thinking how beautiful the light is among the *ocotillos* and *mariposas*? Motels rush by, trailers, tin shacks, pylons, car wrecks, old tire heaps. That's the desert. I bought a case of Coke, I can't stop drinking. I'm thirsty. Reality makes me thirsty.

I was fifteen and I was watching reality encroach on beings like a tragic distortion of beauty. Humanity's trembling aura hovered in the harsh light.

Reality was rushing by, I was diving into humanity. It was a look around at trailers and snack-bars. Reality was a woman in a T-shirt, huge in her breasts, ten times as large with children imprinted onto her loins, onto her thighs. Reality was rushing by skirting fate and destinies. It was a body half-buried under the hood of a car, it was a washed-out pair of jeans, of boots. It was in alternation reality then the desert with long stretches in thinking. Parentheses when approaching cities. Yes, I was fascinated by reality and more precisely by its impossible dimension. Reality is only ever the possible accomplished and as such it fascinates like a disaster or offends desire which would like for everything to exist in its own dimension. I was nothing but a desiring shape in the contour of the aura surrounding humanity. Reality is a becoming spaced throughout memory. There it must be taken by surprise like an essential shape.

A body was required to face the unthinkable and this body, I would produce it, omnipresent at dawn, on storm nights keeping lightning away. I would filter this body of ignorance, of knowledge and of the unthinkable burdening it. This body would be a life equation tapping impossible reality itself.

I was driving, perfect on the edge of solitude. Desiring only the horizon, cacti and a little light as naturally during the day.

It was cold in the desert night and everywhere heat brought beings to life, I trembled about turning reality into an episode by getting close to beings.

CHAPTER FIVE

Longman was under the shower. He enjoyed the water on his head. He liked water running over him. He liked that water was beyond compare on his skin like a mental torture and then his whole body would surrender. He was singing and the water was entering his mouth. Longman would have liked his body muscular. He would have liked to touch that other body, caress its powerful torso, thighs, hard buttocks. He would have felt unburdened of figures and his hunched back would have straightened up ready for the fight. Yes, wrestling body-to-body with other men would have been intoxicating. Longman imagined the muscles straining, the heart throbbing, the veins pumping, the sweat of fear which would not have been like his perspiration during the hours spent doing figures. He would have loved the action and wholly his enemies' bodies. Longman had forgotten the explosion. He had entered the body's instinct fullblooded and his whole being coursed silently through the muscles of the one he would have liked to be. Longman went to the mirror, saw his hollow cheeks and a bad day's stubble. He dressed hurriedly. Outside it may have been daytime but longman did not want to think about it. The curtains were drawn and only the light from the explosion fell upon his movements. Longman did not see the large white envelope slipped under the door.

I could see Angela Parkins again just like the first and only time I had seen her, mouth uttering threats against humanity as if she had had the power to realize them. What did she see, Angela Parkins, when she looked through her theodolite? How did she tolerate heat and thirst, how did she shape her letters, her numbers? How did Angela Parkins make love when she wasn't on the brink of intoxication?

Soon I would be back home and nothing of reality would be changed. Evenings I would watch fear on television. During the day I would watch girls in swimsuits, at night I would listen to their conversations in the bar. During the day my mother would be a woman, day and night, Lorna would be with my mother and I would cherish their winged presence. Sometimes I would take the Meteor. All this time my gaze would be elsewhere turned toward the unthinkable and I would be mindful of everything. I would not faint in the face of reality. I would in no way yield before the tragic aura. Some day I would know the perfect moment of exaltation and indifference in synchrony. Some day I would know the silence and the secret that lives on inside beings so that other civilizations may be born. Beauty was before reality and reality was in writing, open work.

CHAPTER SIX

Longman knew that day was there behind the curtains. He did not feel quite ready for the light of day. He lit a cigarette and picked up the first book he came across. He read like before, calmly. This calmness seemed to want to spread through him but, as he felt it seizing all his limbs, he experienced an opposite cold, mental excitation that made every nerve intolerable in his calm body. His breathing was slow. His entire being was being performed within the limits of the possible. Longman put the book down at the foot of the bed. He spotted the envelope. He got up, parted the curtains, and stared at early morning reality. On the motel lawn, a woman was bending over a watering can. Water was sparking out. Longman leaned over and picked up the envelope.

I had been driving all night. Tucson was just a few kilometers away but I was not yet ready to encounter panic fear again.

I would stop at that motel run by a friend of my mother's. I would tell of my tiredness and need to sleep. She would offer me a room. I would go back to the Meteor for my bag. In the glove compartment the revolver would be hot. I would take out my composition book and the pen. All morning, I would write. The air-conditioner would be noisy. All around me, reality: the see-through curtain, the color of the walls, a superfluous watercolor, a television set, my body still in front of the mirror. I would have the impression of an ultimate understanding of the night, of the desert and of the succession of intimate chances that come up in us like a law of reality. My hand would be slow. Humanity would be unable to repeat itself. I would exist alert in the questioning.

CHAPTER SEVEN

Longman looks closely at each photograph. No doubt about it now, the explosion has taken place and was a perfect success. A photograph is striking evidence. Reality is no longer in longman's head. Reality is in the photograph. Longman is free. There is no more explosion in his head. It's nothing! It's nothing! It's all in the photograph. Longman pins each photograph to the wall. He steps back a bit, moves up. He looks at the explosion. He turns the light on. He turns it off. He opens and closes the curtains. He is seeking proper lighting for the explosion. Then it's as if suddenly the black and white of the photographs were overtaking the room. Longman looks out the window. Outside the lawn is green. There are girls in swimsuits around the pool. Longman lights a cigarette. The whole room is solarized.

Everything is so real around the pool. I entered the life of my fifteen years like a character. Unexpectedly, unsuspecting. All around the pool the light is bright. It contours arms, breasts, thighs, backs, sweeps into eyes. The gaze melts.

A young woman is taking pictures of her two friends. They are posing. They smile but their smiling fades, bleached out by the light. There is always music around the pool. The light is harsh. Eternity begins again at every moment. They laugh as they talk, small talk they exchange in the taste of cocktails. For the pleasure of the tongue. A man comes and sits beside them. He starts a conversation in French. The man is thin. He is wearing a black and white towel around his hips. I can't hear what he is saying. The young women laugh. He gets up and heads for the bar. The light is bright. He returns with a glass of whiskey. He speaks in short sentences. He talks with silence between his sentences. He is not from the area. He is not French. I'm thirsty. I turn my head toward the bar. Somebody dives into the pool. The dripping wet man passes in front of me. He stretches his body out on the towel. The light is harsh. Time wears thin. The girls stir their legs about in the water. I dive in. Reality is a desire spaced throughout memory. Motels are all the same. I am up to my neck in reality.

I will swim a little more butterfly, dolphin, do the frog and do the dog then shower when the tourists leave for a brief outing into the desert, at that hour of the day when everything is so beautiful. When they return I will be at the bar and to reassure herself, the owner will

tell me I've changed a lot 'in all this time,' that I must surely be nineteen by now. Then I will witness the procession of customers coming
to take their place around the tables or at the bar, eyes still in a daze of
mauve and orange.

CHAPTER EIGHT

Longman is reciting Sanskrit poems as he knots his tie. The explosion is far away. The photographs lie amid the equations. He feels light, finally ready to meet the authorities. One last night in this place and he would regain his proud bearing, his charm. He knew how to argue and convince, he would be impeccable. Longman saw his awkward body in the mirror. He put on his jacket and headed for the Bar.

The Bar is filling up. It's a Thursday night. A lot of tourists and accents. Some regulars come and sit directly on the stools set in a semi-circle around the bar. I know all of this.

The desert resolves all plots including the one which behind the eyes solicits invisible humanity on the horizon. In the desert one cannot survive without one's fifteen years of age. One must always be ready for everything, imagine cascades, torrents, the rain, stop the sun and reverse the probabilities in desire. Here in the Bar of the Red Arrow Motel the desert does not really exist. Only thirst which disperses desires, bits of debris in the soul. I grew up in the desert and have no merit in loving it save in the solitude that preserves me from filth.

The man with the accent has just come in. He nods slightly in the direction of the table where the poolside women are sitting. I order a beer. The owner repeats as if to herself that I must surely be nineteen by now. She greets the new arrivals with an air of both welcome and discipline. The music is too loud. Couples are dancing. The corrida of limber bodies and sunburned skins. At the far end of the room, the thin man is leaning against the wall and smoking.

Dawn is a principle which exacerbates energy. I want to understand to excess my desire for dawn, my need of dawn. I order another beer. Somebody touches me on the shoulder. Angela Parkins is there, alert, alive, raw and I am so slow in understanding how much her presence thrills me. She says something trite then goes walking among the tables. The music is too loud. The three women have found partners.

MAUVE DESERT 35

The man from the pool is now sitting at a table with two men. The music is too loud. Nothing is sensuous. Bodies lengthen and cast shadows resembling hair against the girls' faces, arrange their suntanned smiles. Everything is sensuous. Angela Parkins looks in my direction, makes a circular motion in the air with her hand, yes as if she were signaling to me, then points to the dance floor. The music is too loud. The music is too soft. Angela Parkins' body is fanatical, filled with urgency. It leaps like a spirited, capricant animal, flutters and wildly soars, wild Angela Parkins. Eyes are upon our every movement, our every gaze. Beauty is suspended, the beauty that precedes reality, Angela Parkins is singing passionately, half syncing, half live, her mouth rounded by explosive sounds. Her hands swirl above our heads. The palms of our hands, sometimes her hand slides over my hips, sometimes, our acrobatic and aerial fingers clasp one another as if to spin the sense of sounds above our heads, all around us, sometimes her gaze, her cheek.

I don't really know Angela Parkins and yet here we are, bodies close for a moment, then distant, long and slow in the distance of America. We are inseparable and distant in the midst of eternity. We are the desert and *matter* of fact as shadows set. Perhaps the night and the color of dawn. The women have drawn close to us. They seem to be enjoying themselves. The music is too loud. Angela Parkins offers me a drink. 'The same.' Then I stop existing. She is talking, talking, takes off who knows where, she says it starts all over, speech, paths, butterflies and that she just loves words' inevitable slowness, she says that when in distress everything is overcome by the sound of words and that everything then becomes impossible to understand, she says things are exploding in her head and that everything must be attempted again like a backhand, a lob in mindspace, she repeats the mind is fragile but the eyes, but the eyes, Mélanie, she says one must not give up, that nothing is impossible if in the realm of the improbable memory realizes the certitude which in us keeps an eye out for beauty on the horizon, she talks about our attachment to certain words, that they are like small slow deaths in concise reality.

It is half past midnight and the Bar is still full of customers. The music takes hold of everything. Everything is fluid and slow in Angela Parkins' arms. I lack time to understand. There is no more time. Time has entered us in minute detail like a scalpel, time compels us to reality. Time has slipped between our legs. Every muscle, every nerve, every cell is as music in our bodies, absolutely. Then Angela Parkins' body moves slowly. Her whole body is pulled downward. Her body is heavy in my arms. My arms are heavy with the body of Angela Parkins. There is no more music. Angela Parkins' sweat against my temple. Sweat on my hands. Angela, silence is harsh. Angela! A tiny pattern on the temple, a tiny little hole, eyespot. Angela, we're dancing, yes? Angela Parkins has no more hips, no more shoulders or neck. She is dissolving. Angela's eyes, quick the eyes! There is no more balance between us. My whole body is faced with disaster. Not a sound. The commotion all around like in a silent movie. At the far end of the room, there is longman's impassive stare. The desert is big. Angela Parkins is lying, there, exposed to all eyes. Angela is dissolving in the black and white of reality. What happened? He was after all a man of genius. Of course Mélanie is night teen.

Reality, dawn. Furor in the dawn and the galaxies. Policemen, chalk around the corpse of Angela Parkins. The customers didn't see a thing. I didn't see a thing. The desert is indescribable. The gaze melts.

Then came the mauve of dawn, the desert and the road like a bloody profile. There are memories for digging into words without defiling graves. I cannot get close to any you.

A BOOK
TO TRANSLATE

She will never know why her whole being plunged into a book, why for two years she spent herself, stretched herself through the pages of this book written by a woman she knows nothing about except the presumed evidence of an existence cloistered in the time and space of a single book.

All told this book was *innocent*. It rested, thin slice of paper between book ends. It was a December morning, of a spectral whiteness which eroded objects. She was thinking slowness while with her gaze she abstracted the book's equilibrium. And it fell over in the slow motion of silence arousing the throbbing desire that never quit her. Horizontally, the book resembled a tombstone: a name, a title and the cover's brightness.

The universe was a risk. She was a minimal presence, a misted space in front of the window. A marker perhaps between this book and its becoming in another language. This remained precisely to be seen.

Around her everything was noises of the moment, images to conquer. It would have required saying in a single breath. It will require exceptionally many illusions. Like as many appearances, the recourse to some sensorial data she cannot yet claim as hers though dazzled by the nature of the risk.

She would have to name, to converse at length from the inside until perplexed, until the little temptation to translate moved her to the point where one word stretched out taking the shape of an animal or the color in the distance, mauve and, once again in her desire, always to document starting from the horizon surrounding her.

It was possible that none of this could come about unless, by way of detail, she entered the realm of the narrator whose name, Mélanie, let her glimpse a profile outlined against the night.

In this early December as the first snow falls, Maude Laures is gathering all together the clues to her desire and her reading notes which like so many vocal outbursts and days without rain surround the Motel swimming pool. She dives in, is this mistake or strategy, her hand pushing away the first difficulty, the one about which she cannot decide whether it exists because premature or if it is the result of her disparate thoughts. 'It's not true' ceaselessly returns, returning like an intrusion in her notes, cancelling all her efforts at concentration. 'It's not true' returns, restrains her in her world, holds her back from this wild desire which forever lingers, the panic fear of substituting herself to the author of this book. Through an incalculable returning-effect of words, she knew herself to be no longer in a position of absconding from that which, deep under tongue, wanted.

She would also have to emphasize elsewhere the places where feeling had taken her by surprise, from the strange story extract meaning and hold to the uninterrupted act of interpretation. Could she do so without confusing the horizon and the desert, spaces which, by breaking and entering, had come to graft themselves onto her urban world and onto the figures which, inside her, tolerated no disaster? And yet it was with a certain relief that she acquiesced to this book which without warning had undermined her equilibrium, forcing her to apportion her energy so as to include, optimal, the alternative in each word, buried away.

In this early December, her desire is great, resulting from the converged approach and possibility of some transformations.

This morning the sky was blue. She could believe in the disordering of the senses as a mental activity. It was up to her.

She would have liked luxuriant things, a dialogue perhaps in order to illustrate this suppleness of the senses which, at the peak of experience, she felt as an incitement to raving. A dialogue so as to rectify her wariness regarding all characters, her fascination with dawn and especially to cleanse fear of its emotional component. As for the rest, it was enormously an idea. A question of singularity capable of liberating words from their saturation. Everything had nonetheless been possible in the auther's language, but in her own she needed to arm herself with patience. Unfailingly find the fault line, the tiny place where meaning calls for some daring moves. Such was the price of beauty, like a longed-for light. Maude Laures had let herself be seduced, *sucked in* by her reading. It is not always possible to dream without having to follow through on the images.

To apply oneself to understanding, to overlook nothing despite the wanton flow of words. Arouse event. Yes, a dialogue. Force Mélanie into conversation. Sit her down at poolside and make her talk. Put color in her hair, features on her face. Yes, a sumptuous dialogue, an unreasonable expense of words and expressions, a suite, built around an idea, which would drift to the point where Maude Laures would have the time to quietly tour the Motel, to penetrate the mother's and Lorna's room. A dialogue that would allow her, with Mélanie carried away by words, to travel by her side in the Meteor, to open the glove compartment, to touch the revolver, to leaf through the maintenance notebook.

Everything is still just intention to *carry over.* Repeated perspective of the two-way passage. Resorting to the original, nevertheless the intervening process, the drift like a cultural shock, a grave emotion sown with mirrors and mirages.

By night Maude Laures dreamed of *her book* and by day, even before devoting herself to the principles of daring and caution, she would think of Laure Angstelle. Reassured by the knowledge that she was free of everything (she could imagine) about her. Of course she had done some investigating, but had uncovered nothing. Laure Angstelle was the auther of a single book published in a small Arizona town. She could imagine her young or old, free and proud, having perhaps known a great love or a disaster, having been a geometrist or a physicist, still living isolated somewhere between Globe and Gila. Or dead, such was the other perspective.

Images that make it possible to allocate consent. A beautiful flexible machine capable of inverting laughter or despair.

In her sleep Maude Laures sides with perception, though bound by certain sensitive chords to *expression* which she defines as a substantial proposition capable of tipping the scales. She knows it is in approximation that words to begin with. Then amidst the images, she clearly sees that it is *precisely perceived* that the relation establishes itself, assimilates the promoted word or the afterimage.

December is but an aspect of risk. A month scattered across the *Mauve Desert*. A fragile month exploded in Maude Laures' head.

The slightest utterance blocked the jaws. She would then search the wrong side of words, with a hint of panic, the double edge, when the scene seemed too cruel or false to her. Thus she could parallel, albeit briefly, the small sensation that leads to emotion and the meaning that leads to believing. Indirectly *highlight the passage* into her language, accelerate the feeling, with glittering effects, the slippage.

Noon, the snow is still falling. Dreading that which at night skirts the shapes of the great watchful *saguaros,* Maude Laures translates as 'finally the storm rose to subtract reality from the eyes.' Then she dozed off 'in the Meteor, between two songs.'

Laure Angstelle's world was taking place inside her and this quite differently than what she had felt at the outset when, while first reading, she had experienced the diffuse feeling of a reciprocity. Now Laure Angstelle's world had inside her the range of a music all about duration which left her at her work table like a *block of concentration*; her eyes straining over the slightest detail while afar the most intimate images wavered, Maude Laures adjusted to all the intrigues capable, state of alert, of disposing of her fervor ....
.... and

of her coldness. For unexpectedly 'deceiving language' came to her as a necessary reply so that 'the fiction' be reconstituted, the trembled contours of its effects. Maude Laures' coldness was an immeasurable white desert streaked with mauve lightning bolts. Great speed was required in the process so that coldness not be dryness, so that Maude Laures be able to harbor this huge open space, cover every word with another in such a way that the first one not sink into oblivion. Probable modulations. With oblivion, with reply, recover reason.

The time going by was from now on a *time of restoration,* a whole which, like a flower arrangement created by thinking capable of the most mentally precise gestures, exposes itself to having its intentionality reconstituted. Maude Laures felt bound by such an approach and, one heavily snowing morning, decided upon existence among the scenes and the sure symptoms which, in Laure Angstelle's language, had seduced her.

PLACES AND THINGS

THE MOTEL

When arriving by the Phoenix road, it is the first motel on the left with a momentarily blinding metallic roof and a *Mauve* MOTEL neon that resembles a bird about to take flight. Just before the left turn, a slight elevation makes it possible to observe that the motel is built in a ⊓ shape, with a swimming pool in the center of the rectangle and a parking lot which, under the bottom line, borders the road. The Bar is located between the swimming pool and the parking lot. It is accessible from either place. The Bar is painted mauve and contrasts with the whiteness of the building. The neon sign was put up on its roof.

There are six cars in the parking lot around which a little boy is chasing a youth while another, dressed like a sheriff, draws his gun. One of the cars is occupied by a man and a woman. The man is behind the steering wheel, the woman is about to close the door on her side of the car, exchanges a few words with another man, the one heading toward the office carrying a briefcase. The office is to the right of the parking lot. At the entrance, two prickly-pears and an agave create a little green space. The parking lot is not done over in asphalt. A thin layer of dust covers the cacti.

Kathy Kerouac, the owner, is on the telephone, the headpiece cradled between her shoulder and her ear, her hands busy looking for something in a file box. There is a soap smell. At the end of the hallway leading to the rooms in the right wing, a chambermaid is wheeling her cart around.

Kathy Kerouac hangs up, smiles and automatically hands over a blank form to be filled out, takes the form back with the credit card then after a few quick gestures, the key for a moment in suspense over the counter, leans over slightly, points in the direction of the room, of the swimming pool by moving her index finger in a sixty degree angle.

The hallway is dark. On the first door to the right a sign says PRIVATE. A little further to the left, the indoor entrance to the Bar, then the swimming pool behind a glass wall. At the end of the hallway, the chambermaid says a shy *Buenos dias*. The emergency exit is open. At the back, in the light, a man is unloading boxes of toilet paper. He is wearing a peaked cap. He has muscular arms. Out of the half-open truck door blares a blues tune.

The room is large. The curtains are drawn. The window looks out onto a packed-earth area where a teenaged girl, leaning on a rusted barrel, is smoking a little cigar.

THE SWIMMING POOL

Some rooms have a view of the swimming pool. It takes just a push of the sliding door and there is immediately, whitened by the light, a torrid atmosphere, a disappearing world, briefly fossil, a feeling of hyper-reality traversed by the sensation of swayed sense. Here and there a few flies at the water's surface, at the bottom, magnolia petals. All around the pool: deck chairs, two open parasols, a cigarette machine, another for ice. The pool is a place which, whether occupied or deserted, incites nostalgia, that feeling one sometimes experiences when things are desolate and beauty infallibly wins desire over as though it were a matter of living a precious moment.

Every object reflects a harsh light, an evidence of light which exhausts the gaze. And so most of the people who use the pool are soon transformed into pillars of salt, fixed in time, eyes closed, head tilted to eternity, arms and legs heavy producing around the body the impression of an animal species.

A young woman is standing with half her body out of the water, not moving, her gaze vacant. She sometimes lifts her head and eyelids, and her gaze, one might think, is praying to some deity. Sitting at one of the tables near the Bar, a man is reading a newspaper. His legs are crossed, the hair on his chest still smoothed down by the body's vertical movement when emerging from the water.

Some tiles are wet and the pink brightness alternates with the metallic glare of the vending machines, the stairs' chrome ramp. A hose snakes through among the chairs, disappears under the leaves of a flowering agave. The man reading slightly shifts his chair and the sound mix of metal and tile scorches the discrete forenoon. The young woman takes a few steps in the water. Her shoulders, just at water level, are like two reefs around the jade-colored necklace she is wearing.

The atmosphere is restful until Lorna Myher, sudden presence among presences, flings her towel on a chair, flies out over the water, beautiful dive, barely a few drops which for an instant form a prism in the young woman's eyes. Then, as if he could be the cause of this skybow, she *slightly* turns her head in the man's direction who, at this very moment, is stretching an arm down to put the crumpled pages of the *Convention Globe* on the ground.

The young woman has emerged from the water. Light momentarily meets the jade. Lorna Myher's muscular body silently cuts across the pool.

THE CAR

A flash faraway at a distance impossible to assess, like a bone structure, a polished skeleton in the middle of the desert, the thing absorbs all the heat and the attention, attracts and intrigues for in the desert *a thing* means the suspected presence of the human element.

From close up the car is dusty. Its metal body, winged in the rear, in front turns into a bulging outgrowth as though for a repeated frontal approach of the horizon. One of the front tires rests on a large pebble which deforms the rubber already swollen from the heat. The bumper sends back the image of a barrel cactus, especially the red of its flower whose shape close to a rust spot is fraying, rubiginous. The hood of the trunk is covered with inscriptions traced by a finger in the dust.

One of the doors is open. The keys are in the ignition. The ashtray is full of butts, the glove compartment not well shut. A strip of black leather worn by sweat wraps the steering wheel. On the car seat, road maps, a flashlight, a sweater, lizardskin boots misshapen at the little toe on the left foot, a dog-eared book. On the floor by the front seat, a plastic container three-quarters full of water.

Walking around the car (the license plate reads Arizona CHAP 1278), one can see far off the suspected presence of the human element. Someone is there, standing still at the foot of an old *saguaro* whose wound, the woody ribs of the skeleton darkly spot the horizon. It can for a second be mistaken for image or mirage, an illusion as can occur when from moment to moment altostratus formations alter the depth of field and the color all around. But the teenaged girl turns around and can be seen, with a slow step, with a *satiny* step returning to the car, oblivious to the heat, to the inexorable light that transforms lives of flesh into bare bones of narrative.

The car is now heading for Tucson. Its whiteness on the blacktop is absolutely concrete. Until night falls and headlight among headlights, dragon among dragons, it roars in the heart of the heady 'cruising' unfurling on Speedway Boulevard.

Later on in the night, the car is slowly rolling among the organ pipes and ephemeral 'night-blooming princesses.' Night is soft draped around the car, night is white like a silence overexposed under the stars.

THE TELEVISION SET

The television set is in the room adjoining the kitchen. It is the first piece of furniture visible when entering the three rooms converted into an apartment. It is on all day, from the time Lorna Myher wakes up till late at night when Kathy Kerouac, after 'doing her cash,' closes the door behind her and has a last Coke before going to bed.

The television set is beige, covered in cotton lace on top of which a vase of artificial lilies sits permanently; next to it, a tire-shaped ashtray in need of washing, the bottom of which reads EL JOY G RAGE. On either side of the fabric, the varnish is damaged by rings made by glasses. The rabbit ears are turned backwards.

The piece of furniture is massive. Given how it is placed in the room, it becomes necessary all of a sudden, with a skilful hip swing, to get around it. A clumsy move may result in one's flesh getting bruised around the iliac bone.

The screen is always perfectly clear. Never any snow. Seldom is it necessary to adjust the horizontal or vertical hold on the shape and faces of the assassins, the politicans, the *gagsters* who occupy the screen most of the time. Their shape is perfect, one-dimensional, flat. The most visible parts are the necktie and the Adam's apple.

Wherever one stands in the room, the television set attracts attention, transforms the reason for being in the room, be it a pressing hunger or thirst, deflects conversation or disallows it, gives rise to vocal outbursts, especially Lorna Myher's who always comments with great aggressivity and vulgarity on the appearance and physique of the rugby players. It gets even worse during detective thrillers! Her anger unrelentingly smashes down on all the male figures disfiguring the gorgeous landscapes she imagines in women's eyes. Her anger which is first manifested by pacing in front of the set then changes into long incomprehensible sentences alternating with groans. So Kathy Kerouac makes a point of discretely closing the two doors that open one into the office, the other onto the hallway. In her mind there can be no question of scandal.

The television set stays on for hours and hours. During storms this scares Kathy Kerouac and she snuggles into Lorna Myher's arms. Then they converse in profile, eyes worried in view of the images going by, hands knotted as if to exorcise Kathy Kerouac's unspecific fear, the trembling of Lorna Myher's muscular body.

THE TATTOO

The shoulder is suntanned, the skin smooth, the flesh firm. Every twenty seconds the neon lighting hugs the chest, slides over the shoulder, exposes the imago a moment, then moves back up toward the face before fading into the hot night.

The butterfly's wings are open, and the red and mauve and indigo gather around the body prolonging itself, white oval, into the face of a woman with a slow smile like in a Renaissance painting. Then hair or antennae, snakes or spirals, the head ends in a series of curves full of allusions and virtual images as if the artist had wanted to show off her talent or succumbed, despite the needle's slowed motion in the dermis, to a sudden burst of exuberance. One could in fact think that the tattoo had been executed by that woman who lives down south close to the border and who, they say, has tattooed all the 'free spirits' in the area, who, they say, metamorphoses into bird, skull, ship, dragon or flower the shoulders, chests, forearms and backs offered to her expert hands which know how to ease the pain and carefully wipe away the excess coloring and blood at every stage.

There is now a slowness to this night. Voices and laughter can be heard coming from the Bar. They are leaning against the Meteor, Angela Parkins, her head toward the teenaged girl, lips nearing the indelible body. The ocelli are like little apparitions which on the pigmented dermis attract the eye, a sure code for the species.

Angela Parkins suddenly lifts her head as if she wanted to escape an image and this creates the impression that she is about to lose her balance. The girl makes a gesture toward her. At this very moment rain comes crashing down, torrential, curtain; and the violent crackling of water on the cars' bodies, rivulets. Under cover of rain repeated on every surface, night becomes an immense sound allowing things to exist.

Rain on the shoulders is violent. The butterfly glistens all the more brightly but the girl having crossed her arms so that each hand covers a shoulder, the butterfly disappears not before leaving upon Angela Parkins' pupil: death's-head, thorax, sphinx, an impression.

THE REVOLVER

In the first drawer under the counter the object lies on an accounting ledger, its barrel pointed at a one hundred degree angle toward a paper-clip growing a dustball grainy with tobacco. The gunhandle rests on one of the ledger's hard corners.

It has been two years since Kathy Kerouac last used the revolver. Before, she went weekly to the firing range to get to know the weapon, its weight, its range, the trigger's resistance, the thumb's movement when releasing the cock. Now she hardly notices the object when she opens the drawer. Only the weapon's opaque weight when she moves it to take out the ledger gives her the unpleasant sensation of touching a sly animal.

The revolver is always loaded.

When one opens the glove compartment, the revolver glitters every time. It takes up most of the space and its shape reflected in a little make-up mirror amplifies its dimension. The revolver is hot. Some-times it even has to be handled with a cloth or by stretching the hem of a T-shirt so as to make a protective mitten in the cotton.

She rarely uses it but certain days, when everything seems desultory, the teenaged girl can be seen, her back hunched, setting up twenty-or-so empty cans in a semi-circle of three meters' radius around the car. Arm extended, head slightly cocked, one eye closed, the other one sighting through the bead aimed at the cans, she pulls the trigger. In the spring when tarantulas come out in droves, they make fine targets along the open ground.

The revolver is always loaded.

The man carries it in his briefcase. He likes the files to be in order, lying one on top of the other in their folders of different colors. At the very bottom of his briefcase, the revolver as well as a box of bullets can, depending on the thickness of the files, be used as bookends.

In air-conditioned rooms the revolver is cold. The man enjoys the feeling in his clammy hands. He often reads while holding the revolver in his free hand as if the weapon could ensure a permanent coolness in the palm of his hand.

The revolver is always loaded. Not a single mark of ownership distinguishes it from a hundred others seen in gun shops or hanging, as required by law, from storekeepers' belts.

THE BAR

When one enters directly from the parking lot, the dance floor, though small and made of nice blond wood, creates an impression of great emptiness. All around, a dozen or so rectangular black melamine tables in the center of which sits a yellow plastic ashtray, two when the tables are bigger. At the back, the terrace and the pool are partly hidden by a curtain which sharply contrasts the daylight against the dark interior. To the left, the semi-circle bar and, if one takes a few steps toward the middle of the room, the rounded lines of an old jukebox. Behind the bar a huge mirror, liquor bottles, a hanging television set. The screen is on. The volume is on low. When sitting at the bar, back to the pool, one can daydream while looking at the four posters: a storm over Tucson, a field of lupine, cholla cacti in the Santa Catalinas, and the rare spectacle of great *saguaros* under a blanket of snow.

Behind the bar, a woman is busy emptying crates of bottles, filling up the refrigerator, making a list of the stock. The jukebox is blaring. It is the midafternoon lull when the chambermaid starts changing into a barmaid. Her movements are slow. Tiredness is setting in. In half an hour she will loosen her hair, put a little rouge on her cheeks, change her blouse and shoes. Around nine her husband will come and pick her up and Kathy Kerouac will take over. In the car her youngest boy will be asleep, the other two will be silent, the husband will ask about the amount of today's tips.

The woman's gestures are meticulous. Her lips move constantly when she counts the bottles and more strenuously when she writes down the total.

The owner's daughter has just come in through the pool-side entrance. She is wearing a swimsuit, is barefoot and leaving wet tracks behind her. She says hello to the woman and quite naturally her body enters the music's rhythmic sway. Then she heads for the bar and silently watches the woman working. She lights a little cigar. She leans over the counter, stretches the top of her body over so far that she could fall to the other side, pulls out a book.

The girl is deep into her book. The jukebox is now silent. A clatter of bottles and glasses, numbers muttered in Spanish. The hum of the air-conditioner.

A man walks by behind the picture-window which looks out onto the hallway. He stops for a moment, switches his briefcase to his other hand as if it were too loaded, retraces his steps, enters the Bar, orders a whiskey and that the television be turned up. The woman turns up the volume. The man lights a cigarette, swivels his barstool, stares obstinately toward the pool. The girl asks the woman for a pencil, underlines a passage, closes the book, goes around the counter, returns the book to its place, lowers the volume. Kathy Kerouac enters, tells the woman to go and get changed, checks the bills. The man turns around, his gaze glides over the sheet of figures.

CHARACTERS

LAURE ANGSTELLE

It is impossible to say with any accuracy in what city or at what cross-roads for one can all at once imagine her youth in the heart of the desert, in the shadow of the *adobe* houses on Myers Street, or perhaps even think that as an adult she left a large East Coast city to explore her desire, crossing the continent in a few days in her blue Dodge or that she moved closer to the Sonora as years went by after studying in several universities each one having served as a marker in the unconscious journey which had led her toward that great nude on the horizon enticing.

This can be imagined as can seeing her walking along the pure enchantment of the little path winding up into the Catalinas. She must be fifty years old. Her blue eyes spy life all around which like at every dusk lingers in mauve forever. She is holding an old stick found at the bottom of an arroyo, which accompanies each one of her walks at daybreak and at day's end.

One can also think that Laure Angstelle lives in a time-frame that suspends reality, that sometimes reverses it into the dream the same way this can happen with words when, making use of them, one believes one is entering the unspoken of the world and that from there one can, with memory liberated, give desire forms unthought-of till now, capable of subducting us from blindness.

One can believe too that Laure Angstelle knows how to anticipate that moment when the soul *is going to crack* faced with the splendor that is mauve and that all the world's abstraction is going to surge into a word. A studious woman, Laure Angstelle had long since accustomed her body and her thinking to the exercise which consists, very early in the morning, in bringing the cosmos, beings and the 'alphabet soup' of society together in a few swift images. But lest thinking start distinguishing between words, laughter, discourse, the culture medium, she needed silence, to put silence in front of beings like a screen for she knew the price of beauty to be the silence attuning all spheres of sound. Yes, fulfilled, torments or passion, Laure Angstelle's desires had in time clustered into what could properly be called quietude.

Every day at the same time, Laure Angstelle smokes a little cigar. Leaning against her old Dodge she watches the sun carve out the shape of the *saguaros* and darkness snuff out all the visions which the moment before had led her to thinking that darkness is a moment's respite around humanity.

She must be forty years old. Some evenings she can be seen walking in the old quarter of Tucson then taking her car and heading for the Saguaro Bar where two men are waiting for her who talk to her about poetry, to whom she talks about images, acid and dyes, of the texture of paper and of all the problems caused by light. It is of white that they speak, it is of light that she speaks, and this way the voices grow passionate intertwined in the smoke, the lighting and the hum of the air-conditioner.

Perhaps she is thirty years old. Sweat beads her face. She is sitting in the Presidio. She is wearing an eye-catching long red skirt as well as jewellery all around her arms, her neck, hanging from her earlobes. The hair, black, is very short. She is writing in a large notebook. The notebook has a binding and were it not for having caught her in the act and for the whiteness of the pages, one could easily mistake it for a book.

Twenty maybe. She got caught in the rain. She runs to the car. The world is a gigantic wave that hollows river beds, overflows into thirsting gorges and brings the body to yielding, breathless, soaked, sculptured in the light clothing, nipples focused on the horizon.

Now thirteen, sitting at her dust-covered desk, tracing letters and profiles with her index finger on the blond wood that resembles a dance floor.

All of this could be imagined but the questions remained the same when it came to defining the space *Mauve Desert* had occupied in Laure Angstelle's life. Was it autobiographical novel? Had she been at the origin of its publication or had someone in her immediate circle, having read the manuscript, sent it to a printer, with or without her consent? Was this really the only book she had written? For there was nothing precluding the thought that Laure Angstelle was a pseud-onym and that, under her truly name, she had written and published several books. If such was the case, it then became necessary to con-sider the possibility that this book was a climax of sorts, a rupture shrouded in anonymity. Had she perhaps written the book to free her-self from a past, allowing page after page the shallow skin to renew itself through the very balm of sentences, the part changed into mem-ory. Perhaps also had she written out of pure provocation, as a chal-lenge, wanting to feel herself sliding, 'flenching,' irrational, spent; per-haps had she wanted over time to let seep out like an unobstructed story, a part of herself, the undivided part. Perhaps had she never even known the desert and lived in the turbulent atmosphere of a big city still, protecting her solitude and her anonymity so as not to compro-mise her future books or simply to await death's striking edge.

But all of this which could be fantasy in no way invalidated the thought that Laure Angstelle had no doubt been a proud woman with a supple body, eyes filled with torment, vulnerable in the face of beauty and silence, dispirited whenever human misery fell like spittle upon the living.

LORNA MYHER

Lorna Myher had just finished repairing a transmission belt. Her work day would be over in half an hour. She had been working as a mechanic at Helljoy Garage for two months now. She was just about to light a cigarette when she saw a car coming, a Meteor, driven by a woman. The pump attendant went over but the woman said the motor needed looking at, maybe the fan belt or the alternator.

Lorna Myher had grown up in the city of Ajo a few miles from the copper smelter. She was an only child and lived with her mother and grandmother in a trailer-home bought by her father shortly before his death. Every day a great plume of poisonous smoke stopped time over the city and Lorna Myher turned her head southward to the Ajo Range. Only there could she feel herself a creature among creatures, watching for the slightest sign of life, following every trace liable to lead her to a den, an anthill, a nest. She loved those moments when holding her breath she became scales, pearls, claws, felt her supple body capable of any camouflage amidst the thorns and wild berries.

The pump attendant pointed in Lorna's direction but the two women had already charted a movement drawing them closer. Lorna wiped her hands on her jeans and, as though at the back of her gaze this was about getting acquainted, held out her hand to Kathy Kerouac who simultaneously startled by the gesture and by the skin's roughness without realizing it applied a slight pressure of the palm. Lorna's eyes turned to the car. She opened the hood and her hands found their way among the pistons, cylinders and greasy cables.

Lorna Myher was walking along a ledge of *ocotillos*, once again she had taken advantage of recess to elude the young schoolteacher's green gaze and the jumble of letters and numbers which somewhere inside her clashed with a will to silence, a fierce need of the senses. It had rained all that night and there was a strong smell of creosote. She turned around and saw that a girl from her class was running toward her. Lorna Myher waited a moment then when the girl reached her, at that distance when breaths can intermingle, kissed her on the mouth. The girl closed her eyes. Lorna's gaze slid over the lacquered green leaves of a creosote bush, swept into the scarlet and sweet taste of the flowers all around.

Lorna straightened up and said the car would have to spend the night in the garage. As Kathy Kerouac hesitated, Lorna offered to drive her home in her jeep. While riding Kathy Kerouac talked about the Motel and about her daughter Mélanie who would soon be five years old.

At fifteen, Lorna Myher had finished with school. She now spent most of her time in the snack-bar at the factory where her mother worked. Across the street was a garage young bikers used for repairing their machines. After several warnings and a fight from which she had emerged the winner, Lorna was allowed to circulate freely among the tools and motors. Little by little the soot, the sweat, the dust and the vulgarities drove back into her memory the mountainside and the orangey red of flowering *ocotillos*.

Lorna parked the jeep and let the motor idle. Kathy Kerouac then offered the prospect of a drink by the pool. Two or three things to take care of first and she would be right with her. Lorna looked at her jeans and t-shirt and asked where she could change. When Kathy Kerouac joined her by the pool, Lorna was wearing shorts. The white of her thighs contrasted with the dark tan of her face and arms. Lorna was watching a little girl playing in the water with a large plastic dolphin.

Lorna Myher was twenty years old when for the first time ever she saw waves. It wasn't the ocean, it wasn't the ocean at Big Surf but Lorna Myher experienced such a frenzy when she saw this gigantic pool with its thousand whirlpools that wave after wave she let herself be carried by the black and yellow mattress which, magic carpet, gave her the impression she could swim, that she could do anything like that fabulous creature the green-eyed teacher had talked about one day. From then on Lorna Myher couldn't live without water. Mornings and evenings she went to the pool and soon could be seen cutting through, butterfly or dolphin, the chlorinated water.

Lorna accepted Kathy Kerouac's invitation. During the meal the little girl spilled a glass of milk. They talked about a myriad marvels, about the month of May and the moss atop the mountains which sometimes gave the impression that the desert could be conquered.

This Lorna Myher remembered as if it had been yesterday. She looked at Kathy sleeping soundly, one arm under the pillow, the other lying along her hip. Lorna got up without a sound, then as she headed for the kitchen, turned on the television.

KATHY KEROUAC

Kathy Kerouac's voice was in itself a presence, a sound sequence of space and time which like perfume wafted through the rooms, the hallways, the apartment. The entire Motel was permeated with her grave and melodic voice, a voice which, when no attention was payed to the words, could bring to mind a motet. Every vibration of the vocal chords gave the impression of a sound originated in multiple mouths. No matter what the situation, the voice adapted itself and what was urgent, was, what was comical became so and what could threaten would take shape behind the voice's veil.

Kathy Kerouac knew the power of her voice. It was, she said, her 'golden thing,' an amulet protecting her against all disorders of the spirit. Her voice was a charm that could stop violence and transform crudeness into courtesy, foolishness into finesse. So Kathy Kerouac was under the impression that nothing was ever *altogether* dangerous, the feeling that no word spoken could soil her world.

Given that her voice had such an effect on living beings, Kathy Kerouac did not always pay attention to what she said. Because for her the merit of words was in producing that resonance which deep in the throat had her tuning the most beautiful instruments, hearing the most faraway harmonies. She would choose her words for the length of the vowels, the mimic of the lips that could, if the breath, if the tongue sought to, reproduce the maddest laments and imitate, this being the case, her sense of worry.

It was through her voice, as if it could act as a screen, that Kathy Kerouac contemplated the obscure language linking her to Lorna

Myher. To contemplate was indeed the verb, for she could then spend hours, absorbed by the movement of active and passive voices, their meeting points and breaking points, trying to understand what in the rhythm could produce such a degree of tension, such an alternation of desire and emotion.

Whenever Lorna came very close, Kathy Kerouac would wrap her voice around her and Lorna would silently sojourn in the contrast of words leaving it up to the little flashes blinking in her gaze to round out the sound shapes that made her long for Kathy Kerouac. When Kathy talked that way, the television would sink into the distance like a washed-out form of civilization.

For Kathy Kerouac thinking in silence was unthinkable, an unsteady shape in the machinery of body and soul grappling with life. She needed resonance, an answer, an echo to the sounds she produced. So she spent a good part of her day on the telephone. Everything was a pretext, be it groceries to order, a reservation to check, some crisis forcing her to cancel her shooting practice. Thinking in silence was nonetheless a reality to which she was sometimes compelled. Had she not many times fled the sound of her own voice and withdrawn into an obtuse silence when Mélanie came home at dawn or when it would have been necessary to talk more at length about men and the desert? She knew it, the risk would have been too great of a lament or of a huge uproar in her voice making her lose control of it.

Kathy Kerouac was said to be a serious woman, honest and discrete, but all this was said because Kathy Kerouac's voice dissipated any arrogance, any anger like a siren's song. The child's father was said to be an actor who had once worked in Old Tucson. A 'rough-mannered' woman was said to be living permanently at the Mauve Motel. Mélanie was said to have coarse manners. All of this was heard to be said but Kathy Kerouac always found a way of saying that her own mother had known the land and that in the heat she had toiled, shrub, brustling, muffled children's cries, across the fields, in the plain, 'rough-mannered, rough-mannered' among the furrows, the panic grass and the crazy fern folding under the tractors for the devastation was great, O great devastation, said Kathy Kerouac, tears in her eyes and her voice headlong, ready to remake the world.

Kathy Kerouac's voice was a space on the horizon. It could crackle, torrential downpour or sand storm, stretch out like a skein of approvals or isolate an invested sentence in the maze of boredom.

Yet the voice could *take fright.* This Kathy Kerouac foresaw only too well when syllables suddenly started coming out of her mouth like little fragments of oblivion giving her the impression she was contradicting herself. It was in these moments, when words were both true and false, solemn and light, on the tip of the tongue and deep in the throat, that space shrank in her mouth like a hard-felt blow.

Yes, Kathy Kerouac though proud of her voice knew how to pinpoint the moment when her own voice could dissolve into disorder and chaos or start suddenly to shimmer like a naked female body, the extended nape of a neck. She always knew to stop there in the image and the words.

Such was the ordeal of Kathy Kerouac who gave everyone the impression of being a woman without expression.

ANGELA PARKINS

For almost twenty years now Angela Parkins had worked as a geometrist. Dryness and sun had long since etched her face. Her bright eyes accustomed to perspectives of all kinds were of a black capable of dimming the misleading reflections the desert's white light poured into her calculating gaze. Her habit of precision had made her a determined woman, capable of representation and having a sense of territory, a large territory covering several *states.*

Her team had been working close to Death Valley Junction for the last few days and she had decided that tonight she would go to the Amargosa Opera House, that little theatre lost amid aridity and impregnable dunes which, like a strange fruit cut out on the horizon, evoked that appetite of spectacle beings develop when nostalgia burdens the spirit.

The day stretched out into tracings, volumes and surface areas. The heat was unbearable. Bodies dehydrated in a few hours. Angela Parkins never thought of protecting herself. She was carefully writing her report while the men prepared to return to Death Valley Junction.

The hall is very small. On the walls, spectators' boxes have been reproduced, gilt balconies crammed with Spaniards in sixteenth-century costume. In the first row women whispering, a handkerchief, a fan in their hand. The red and blue of the dresses, bosoms all of flesh, strange headdresses, everything that shapes a civilization when one looks at the expression deeply in the eyes. Wasn't it the expression in the gaze that made it possible to distinguish between the tools, the weapons and the ornaments, how death could be vanquished, how

women, slaves among slaves, could in their rounded form be party to
life? Wasn't it from the gaze that one could discern the use of speech
and observe as on a topographical map, thoughts, their depth, the lev-
eling-out, the little details making it possible to measure the distance
covered by the thinking spirit?

Angela Parkins loved spectacle. All spectacles, everything that could
offer itself as a volume in the mind, turn dialogues into intrigues or
make the soul clamor in eternity. She loved for bodies to be occupied
by passions or for them to express passions' cliches, adopt poses un-
equaled by any animal. For Angela Parkins the body was *stricto sensu* a
matter of sensation, chaos, atom, vivid flesh. Yes, she also loved faces
but a face is always so complex and features can in a few seconds transform themselves, so easily misleading like beautiful masks, spread terror, throw the soul into the deepest distress.

She loved extreme feelings, explosions of joy, of voices, sudden
rushes of tenderness making the body levitate, speech that is luxuriant,
abundant and raw for, she believed, the body must be voracious and in
the same breath be able to fly off as capricious and ductile as a silk
thread.

The performance was about to end. The ballerina would go and
change her clothes, put on her jeans and snakeskin boots. Voices
would meet for a moment at the exit and Angela Parkins would be
back in her motel room lost in the depths of immensity.

The room would be plain, the walls beige, the pool deserted. Angela
Parkins would open a recent book and try like every night to forget the
image of hell, forcing back into her mind the first explosion, the huge
tear in the trembling atmosphere, the animal's flanks under her thighs,
her fall from the horse, the horse at full gallop, the grass against her
cheek, a monarch fluttering over an acacia flower. In the distance, hell.

Angela Parkins put the book down at the foot of the bed. Her eyes
stared at the wall. What is truth? *Aletheia, aletheia.* She was like a witness-mound that has escaped erosion, isolated spectator, proof. Angela
Parkins fell asleep, her body tight, as stiff as a suspicious shape under
the sheet.

Tomorrow it would be necessary to wait for dawn before heading

out to Arizona again. The road would be long. The men would talk
about equipment, about the latest things. Their words would seem
plausible. There would be the rabbits' eyes, little glimmerings under
the headlights. Then all would fall silent and Angela would take the
wheel. Dawn would be dazzling, unspeakable in mauve. Then once
again whiteness would make reality falter and the raw feeling of hyper-
reality would overtake things. In Tucson the wheels would stop at the
first motel on the left.

Longman

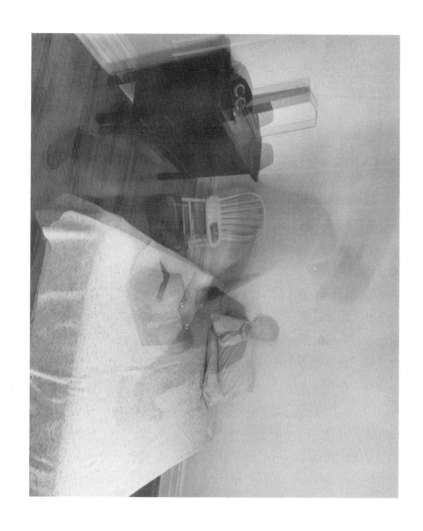

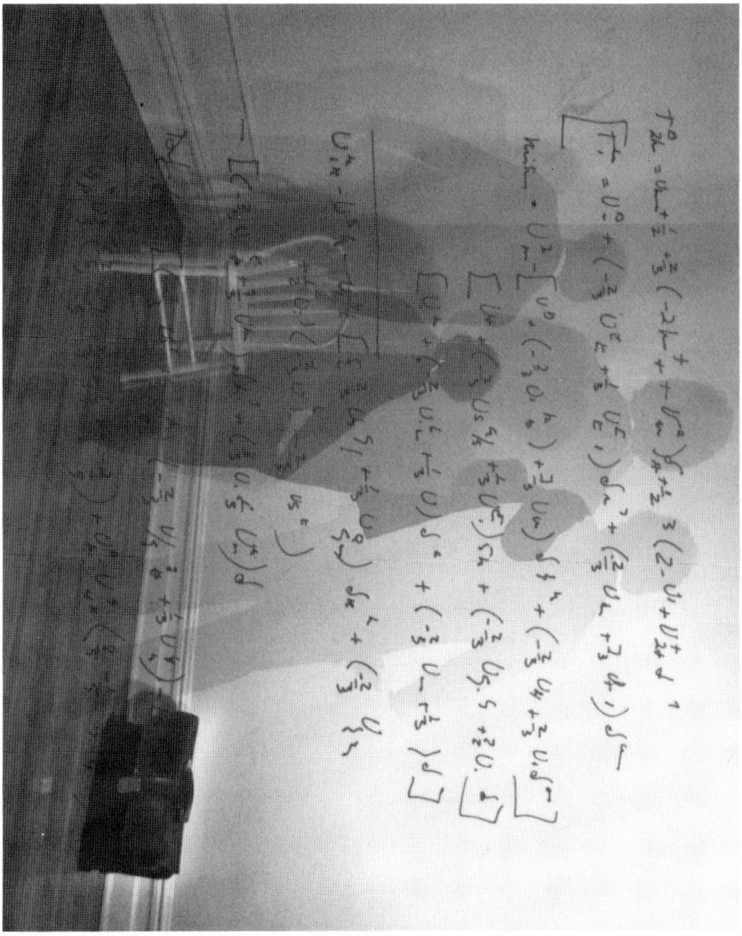

MÉLANIE

At once Mélanie's face takes its place in the story as a recurring figure, a few undecidable features of solitude although in some respects, when the face is attentive, one may question the very composition of the appearance. For living fast in the present assigns certain features their site: wrinkle, scar, at the very heart of smoothness, the present naturally appropriates thoughts as a whole, opens and closes skin, apportions desire, hope and violence, circumstantial marks anchoring the face to existence.

Mélanie's face like an image following its course between the narrating voice and the character, this face opens up chasms of comparisons. Like any face, Mélanie's is a physical act on the part of thinking. It mimes, simulates, plays, trembles, frightens, charms, contrasts, it retains or rejects through each one of its pores what is true, the feint, the image, the superstition of living, it acquiesces, attests, it denies until the facial muscles regulate the tension, adjust the inner avid strengths and cumulative pressure of reality. When the face offers itself, the short hair and bare forehead, the fine brows, the perfect symmetry are what give desire its configuration. When on the contrary the face insists on wanting more, the mouth harbors such velocity that both lips and chin can very clearly be seen mounting the offensive. If the eyes intervene, they draw shadows, figures, holes like great negations, suspend themselves over emptiness or else start dancing around some hypersexed images. But most often the eyes, when they begin listening, successively line up the thousand details of speed and light converged.

Though young it is a lived-in, multiplied face, not common but bearing the mark of what amply fills the senses and thereby renews their theatricality: the multiple of dying, the multiple of passion. It is a face one could describe as competent, meaning capable of compensating in a worthwhile manner the inexperience of the features with some subtle inner stagings which result in wrinkling the forehead, stretching the mouth, lifting the eyebrows, hollowing the right cheek slightly, all of this in order to correctly dose out the vulnerability, wholesome looks and caprices lodged in Mélanie like contrasts.

The face is a likeness, neutral and distant, capable of softening reality. Nothing psychological, only the intensity, rush of intensity, concentrated speed of a rough-mannered desire to say. If this face were to be described, the features would have to be gone over a hundred times, the curve of the nose, the signs, the chapped lips creating the impression of great thirst and that the voice no doubt also cracks in the dry air. One would have to emphasize the length of the eyelashes, the light down on the cheeks, proceed in such a way that the face could state on what conditions it chooses to exist. In the interval, summer's showy play of colors repeated like a single season on the skin's golden grain would be in full light, a constant. In shadow the face would have only to be pronounced absent or consigned to silence with a mouth haunted by the noise of civilization.

Thus, although young, Mélanie's face does not deceive. One can look at it and think nothing, one can discreetly desire that it become animated for the duration of a dialogue, one can want to turn it into a mask and wear it when the taste for living exceeds in us good measure and that forehead, jaw and lips are plotting a few attempts on reality.

SELF-PORTRAIT OF MAUDE LAURES

You are there, arms extended, knees bent, eyes straight forward. The ball starts to soar. Your gaze never leaves it, yet the blue of the sky, the treetops, at the end of the park, the green blurs for a moment, the light bright in your eyes. You hit the ball. It speeds into the net, rolls like a little head. Your opponent attempts a smile. You feel the sweat on your neck, in your hair, along your temples. You lick your lips, a salty taste. You would like to be 'fast so fast.' You concentrate. You raise your arms. The ball is a bird. You are as taut as a bow. You volley with all your might. Your body is an oblique. Your body pivots. The ball goes across. Your hand slips on the leather handle. You think of the steering wheel. You reply with a drop shot. The ball lands like a lightning-struck animal. You watch your opponent. You would like to anticipate her every move. You strive to understand the why of those short chapters that give longman a fictional character. You move up to the net. Your smash is successful. You think of Lorna's muscular body. You hear her bitching in front of the television set. You swallow your saliva. You reply with an easy lob. You win your serve. The sun is in your eyes. You would like to leave for some faraway place, to dissolve in the heat. The ball brushes your shoulder. You lose your balance.

You change the rhythm. You force her to play in the back court. You keep her at a distance. You watch her foot moves, the movement of her wrist, the gaping of her shirt. Her hair is a flaming red. Her gestures graceful. She must be twenty-five, thirty perhaps. She raises her arms. Her chest lifts. With every serve she breathes noisily as if the blow were going to strike, fatal. Her defensive moves are risky after all. She moves toward the net. The game is over. You both smile. You walk together along the little green path until you reach Joyce Street. You go home. You open a beer. On your writing table you spread the file folders you have prepared for each character. Maude Laures, tell me, what can possibly happen on this hot and desultory July afternoon? Say, what can be plotted in your gaze that you were unable to understand during the initial readings when you annotated this unusual book found in a second-hand bookstore? Tell me how this 'innocent' book came into your life interrupting your studious woman's routine, double-exposing the portrait in you for, you know very well, Maude Laures had been teaching at a girls' school for three years. She was liked by her students and the administration appreciated her enthusiasm in communicating, her pedagogical approach. She never talked about politics and the books she put on the course list could only lead to the pleasure of reading. She was not known to have a lover, husband, or woman love. She surrounded herself with fine objects. Lamps, tables, chairs were for her sculptures, marble, beautiful smooth and cold surfaces which helped her think. At Christmas she went south. After Easter holidays she talked about the Citadelle, about the British on the Plains of Abraham, the beauty of the St. Lawrence River and always her voice caught fire like leafage in October. When September came her hair was always very short. She had stopped wearing eye makeup when she started wearing contact lenses. On payday she would buy five or six books, reading them she knew would reassure her about existence or somewhere deep inside comfort the hazards of her thoughts. 'Love books,' she constantly repeated to her students, 'for you never know by what chance encounter, at the turn of a phrase your life can find itself transformed.'

On winter evenings, Maude Laures took long walks. Sometimes stopping in a small café on Bernard Street, talking for a long time with the waitress from Rivière-du-Loup. When there were too many customers she would sit at a table where she could watch people going by in the cold and look at the small reliefs on the facade of the Outremont Cinema.

Though she was often between the four walls of her apartment,

Maude Laures liked the raw sound that accompanies reverie when one plunges into the city with its multiple outrages and devices. Despite her absentminded air, nothing escaped her of the signs and fires that stoke enthusiasm or which, to the contrary, inhibit all perspective in the great rectangle of solitude which acts as a screen for urban chests.

For Maude Laures, life was composed of three things: avoiding all confusion between men and reality, isolating paradoxes, following through on her most impudent thoughts. Yet it was not an easy task for always a need for images and colors arose which simultaneously compelled her to the simple beauty of dawn and to that baroque laughter she knew could hurl stones at everything, *matter* of fact and certitude.

And now, tell me Maude Laures, what can possibly happen on this sultry afternoon as you prepare to switch roles, to risk the desert with Laure and Mélanie, to stretch out, when night has come on the naked ground, eyes on the alert while the Taurids shoot by and as, in the ancient tongue which is yours, you are still imagining scenes?

SCENES

I

Time begins again between Kathy Kerouac and Mélanie. Faces make an effort and lips and the gaze's slant can be seen obliquing their way through words. The heat is high, the pool water blinding.

– It's vague, an effort suffices, or a few words said, or else seeing you in front of this television set.
  – It's vague! And yet there are words for saying what you're feeling.
  – You look at Lorna and see nothing else around.
  – My gaze is wide.
  – Vague. You don't see me.
  – I see what I love, what is reason to live. You're the center core of my existence. You have no idea what goes on inside me. Do you think my thoughts are free of your face, of all those memories that settle in our memory over the years?
  – Anything to avoid the present, right? But don't worry, I'm leaving. You're both too present and too absent. You exist too strongly inside me because you never talk to me. I'm forced to imagine your tenderness, to invent dialogues in which you tell me of your love, your esteem, your appreciation. But I'm weary of these fantasies. I don't want to spend my life in emotional disorder. I want the horizon very clear before me.

– A girl does not go out into the desert to feed on the sun and the horizon. A girl must not go as far as where the eye is misled.

– My gaze will be vigilant. I'm alert in the questioning state.

– The sun, the heat, the solitude will overcome you.

– The heat originates inside me. I know how to be alone. If only you could imagine in my eyes the splendor of existing!

– You mean that your gut wants to speak.

– I'm saying that my eyes are speaking about existing.

– Your eyes are so full of arrogance and pride that they will necessarily mislead you. Don't you know that …

– No, I don't know anything. I'm leaving because you don't teach me anything. You watch that television. Your attention turns only to Lorna. No, you don't teach me anything.

– You know, eyes, oh! you'll know soon enough.

– What about eyes?

– Eyes that seek to get ahead of the horizon. Impatient eyes will always be disappointed.

– I will be bright and patient.

– There is no outsmarting them. Eyes need to think and when they're thinking, we must yield. Eyes cause the faces they penetrate to crack. You too will yield.

– I'm not afraid of death.

– Mélanie, you mustn't think about death. Death is something somewhere invented by men to forget and to elude reality.

– Don't be ridiculous. Death is an encounter for everyone.

– I'm saying that men invented death because they think about it. They cultivate it raucously.

– Have you never thought about death?

– I became mortal the day I gave birth to you. Death does not come toward us, it's we who in time *quite naturally* go toward death.

– Why are you talking to me like this now?

– I've always wanted you to be able and whole.

– I am.

– Yes, because that's how I wanted you to be.

– You'd like to be everything, wouldn't you? Everything to me, everything to Lorna, everything to your customers. You'd like perfection to begin with you. You'd like to wipe the slate clean, make believe. Reinvent the world and the law.

– I want peace, the end of massacres and forgetting.

– *You are merely a mother.*

– You think a daughter can dictate things to her mother that could make her 'easy'! A mother is never 'easy.' A mother makes all the difference in a life.

– A mother makes a difference if she has taught her daughter well. A mother who doesn't teach her daughter deserves to be forgotten in front of her television set. An ignorant mother is a calamity.

– I taught you through my gestures and my courage.

– It was Lorna who taught me how to swim, how to know the desert. All you wanted to teach me was how to cry. I learned about fear from looking at you. You seem afraid of everything. But what is a life if one is afraid of everything?

– I guess you can go now. We have nothing more to say to each other. Take this silver comb. It will bring you luck and happiness.

– Happiness! It's your looking for happiness that bothers me.

– I'm looking for contentment, well-being, daily wellness.

– Comfort. You're looking for convenience, facility.

– Mélanie, you should leave or keep quiet because you don't know what you're saying. You're violently confusing words, you're appropriating them as though they were sugar-cubes you were placing on your tongue and waiting for them to take effect. Forgive me if I've been unable to teach you. I believed that I had. Despite your refusal to talk, your constant running away. I thought my affection was enough, that my voice somewhere inside you could reach the hard knot you have for a soul.

– What becomes knotted in the heart is knotted with the silence of others. You know, *your voice,* your beautiful voice never really spoke to me. Your voice just superimposed itself on the mediocrity which in this Motel precludes all hope. I'm leaving but you know I'll be back. I'll come back because I know you'll be expecting me. You see, our eyes are dry. That's a good thing. Never cry for me. Never do that because then your tears would join with mine and we would be carried away, yes, I believe we'd both be carried away by a single wave.

II

Two hours were all it took for dailiness to become a small dark spot in the consciousness. Kathy Kerouac and Lorna Myher parked the jeep. Vertical section on the horizon, their bodies form a certain presence in the mauve.

– Hurrying up, slowing down. It seems we're either too heavy or light, or does the desert create this impression of confounding the body's real weight?

– By your side I keep my balance. You are this high-density water which keeps the body afloat and keeps it from sinking deep into the whirlpool.

– Do I deserve to be so valorized and celebrated? I'm just an ordinary woman.

– And I'm a great dyke fulfilled with joy by your side. You see, all we need is to get away from that Motel for awhile to come alive again.

– We need to leave that damned television set alone.

– You are ...

– Don't tell me who I am, even if what I am I can only discover with you.

– Because I'm like you or because we're different?

– Because you're lively and afraid of nothing. Yet [*discomfort in her voice*] you really should learn to read.

— You still can't accept me as I really am. I'm a body. A body happy when in water. Have you never thought that my body would disintegrate if ever it entered the twisted stuff of words? If you only knew how much I prefer my own nimble fingers a thousand times over all those fragile lines a thousand times twisted which men write, which your daughter writes.

— But everyone around us knows how to read and write.

— Everyone around us doesn't do, doesn't think, doesn't bite their shelove's ear like we do. No one around us does what we do. No one feels what we feel.

— I'm an ordinary woman and I feel like others feel.

— Others, who? Poor Kathy, my love. Poor me, your shelove. What will we become if you don't love me as I am, if I want you as you are not? How many caresses, how many times hands over our mouths, how many times the belly's fire before we become exactly what we are? Or is that irrelevant?

— But reading is something necessary. Reading is food.

— Yes! 'What are we eating? What are we eating?' Your daughter often says that. And she runs away, your daughter. As for me, I devour. I take. I don't wait for the twisted lines to make my body breathless and unfit to the point where it can't tolerate good tastes and beautiful images. Your daughter talks about eternity too much.

— My daughter is subtle. She understands things.

— And I'm gross, I suppose! Tell me what you're doing with me then.

— With you I do what's essential. My life. I invent my reality. I outline certainty and weave my faith.

— That's all very abstract. [*Silence*] Do you think it possible to love around the body? To love without smells, without taste, without tongues seeking their salt on the beloved's skin, without the rustling of hands on thighs, without needing to refine our senses? Do you think you could have loved me without considering my body, if I had been just an image at the back of your eyes, if you had had to leave out my body to choose me?

— Yes, I think I would have loved you even never having found your body. Yes, I could have loved you and left out your body.

– But leaving out my body, who would you have loved?

– I would have loved the impossible in myself, even till it bruised me.

– And you would have done it anyway?

– Anyway.

– You disconcert me. I find it unbearable, even for a second, to think of loving without bodies coming in to free or to sustain desire.

– Who said anything about desire? I'm talking about a specific emotion which creates presence way beyond the real body.

– Emotions, we have more than we need to elude reality. Desire is what prompts every encounter, every life impulse.

– I don't desire you. I'm moved by you. I'm keenly touched by everything in you that signifies. That is infinitely more precious than desiring you. I'm vitally touched by you.

– As for me, I say desire and quickly, bodies one on one. Bodies of abundance, caresses, embraces, excitation. I want traces, marks, blood streaming in our veins. Love needs evidence. Carnal evidence other-wise the body languishes, dissolves into the twisted stuff of words, the chaos of emotion.

– Emotion is what pacifies.

– So you don't desire me? In that case what are we doing together? How am I different from what stirs your emotion?

– You are unique.

– No I'm not, and you know it. Nobody is that free. No one woman is that alone in the world.

– Well then I guess there's no explanation and that it's pointless to seek a reason for the love I feel for you. Perhaps it's easier to choose from among the suite of mirrors, costumes and roles, words that are simpler, softer, less crude, ordinary.

– When it comes to love, one mustn't be ordinary. It offends me to hear you say that you're an ordinary woman.

– You mean it humiliates you to love an ordinary woman.

– I don't think you're ordinary. But yes, it humiliates me to hear you say it. I spent my whole childhood, my adolescence refusing to become an ordinary woman. We were poor but to my eyes that was no excuse for being confined to the ordinary. Look at your daughter, she isn't ordinary either. And you may be sure that that has nothing to do with knowing how to read or not.

– You're giving words quite a turn.

– Can one exist without turning words into sentences!

– You see, you're more twisted than you care to admit.

– I'm in love. I'm doing everything I can not to lose you. For me this goes without saying and without drama.

– Yet terror is everywhere. Ice, the sparkle of cold laughter.

– This isn't something we can prevent. Terror is. We can't escape this cloud. Wired, revolted or resigned, we walk in its wake.

– Can we constrain the story?

– The narrative of our lives, of terror or of the impossible?

– Merely sum up. Quite simply. Without violence, with a few markers along the way.

– We have no markers but ourselves. We are surrounded by signs that invalidate our presence.

– Well then let's say that I would like for us to sum up our presence. Lorna Myher, you great dyke from Ajo, send me into raptures. Adventure me in desire. Do everything that you must, that you mustn't, my trust is absolute.

– I will do only what in you desires. That's the only presence I can offer you.

III

The shoulder is suntanned, the skin smooth, the flesh firm. The neon lighting hugs the chest, slides over the shoulder, exposes the imago a moment, then moves back up toward Mélanie's face.

– It's a beautiful night.

– Night is what allows sudden changes.

– Night is concrete.

– Night is oblique. On one side beings, on the other side beasts. This is why we tremble, when night has come, about not finding our place.

– Here we are, speaking to each other quite naturally and yet, Angela Parkins, I know nothing about you.

– I come from the desert.

– What do you know about the desert, the sun and men? My mother says that ...

– The desert is a space. Men came there one day and claimed that this space was now conquered at last. They claimed they suffered over their conquest. They suffered because the desert suffers no error. But men confused error with suffering. They concluded that their suffering could correct the error of nature, the very nature of error. This is how they hooked into death.

– It's a beautiful night.

– Night is always beautiful for it forces us to feel with our skin and our inner eyes. At night we can count only on ourselves.

– Night is beautiful in sheer solitude but your presence makes this night even more real for me.

– Night is strange.

– That's because the body changes rhythm.

– At night it is especially necessary to wait for the body to change its trajectory in the universe. To move in such a way that all of our senses can transit freely. Capture the vast emptiness. How old are you?

– I hope I never become like other people.

– How do you know you haven't already?

– I know.

– I'm thirsty. How long have you had the butterfly tattoo on your shoulder?

– A month. It gives me strength for facing reality. It gives me wings. I'm Sagittarius. It makes me feel like somebody put their hand on my shoulder, looked at me, taught me.

– Taught you what? You really want to be taught about life?

– You no doubt desired that once.

– I made my own way. I don't owe anybody anything.

– Do you think that's the way to find joy?

– I'm thirsty. I spend hours and hours resisting thirst. Waiting for sunset. I spend my life watching the horizon in detail. I've never given happiness a thought. I charge ahead. I troat.

– Do you know that animal?

– Which animal?

– The stag. They say it is often compared to the tree of life and that it symbolizes rebirth. For the Pueblos it represents cyclical renewal.

– Mélanie, what are you talking about?

– What I've read.

– Come closer. Let me get a good look at this butterfly. It has the thorax of a great sphinx.

– Well?

– *Nothing.* Why did you say that night changes the body's rhythm?

– Because it's true. Do you think I would have dared to follow you and speak to you in broad daylight?

– During the day I'm far away, way off in the vastness. During the day all my attention is focused on the earth's crust.

– Don't you want to be loved?

– I'm not lovable. My thirst is too great. Mélanie, you're very young. Your mother is probably already worried about your absence.

– My mother knows me. She knows that night and day I feel the need to run. To always go a bit beyond myself to let reality loose.

– I think we look alike.

– Without a mirror it would be hard to tell.

– I think our eyes are better able to tell when there are no reflections.

– There, I'm close to you. Do you recognize me?

– Yes, I recognize you. It's true that you are ageless. You have always existed. Don't go thinking that I'm making things up. I can tell among the signs and the clues what in you is made to last. You needn't fear time. Only speed will damage you.

– Don't say that. I love living fast.

– That's what I recognize in you.

– Rain.

– Stay just a little longer. Rain can only soften our lips and make the night palpable.

– The rain on your lips is fine.

– 'We pray thee send forth rain, blessings, immortality.'*

* Veda.

IV

The scene can be imagined by parting the curtain between auther and translator. The distance is abolished by imagining the two women sitting in a café. One is smoking and so is the other. Both like dealing with silence but each one here is looking to understand how death transits between fiction and reality. The language spoken is the auther's.

– I feared for a moment that you wouldn't come.

– Here I am. Don't worry, I took great *pains* to be here.

– I have no rights. You come before me.

– What do you want from me?

– To hear what I can make my own. Everything you tell me will be...

– Useful?

– Necessary. I've been living with this book for two years. I've only just recently conceived the project of translating it.

– What would you like to talk about?

– One thing only: Angela Parkins' death. I'd like to talk to you exactly the way I imagine Angela Parkins would if she could get out of character, if she were its ultimate presence.

– I'm listening.

— Why did you kill me?

— You're going fast, Angela, you're getting too directly to the heart of the essential. Wouldn't you rather we talk first about you or about me, that somewhere we find the familiar Arizona landscapes again? [Silence] *So be it, if you like, we can talk about your death right now. But first, swear to me that you didn't see anything coming. Swear it.*

— Saw what coming? Love, death? Saw what coming? Mélanie or the assassin?

— Saw reprobation coming.

— What! You would have punished me for what I am.

— I'm not talking about you. I'm talking about everything around you. Intolerance. Madness. Violence.

— In that case I saw nothing coming. Certainly I saw myself lost, delirious, wary and minotaur, drunk and arrogant, joyous and casual, nostalgic and in love but I never saw that man's madness coming.

— And yet you knew him.

— I knew him by reputation. He was an inventor, a great scholar, but how could I ever imagine that that man carried such hatred inside him?

— You never noticed anything in his ways, in his gaze?

— He looked normal. He looked like a normal client. To tell you the truth, I never noticed him. My whole being was involved in the rhythm moving me closer to Mélanie.

— Well then I'll tell you. I'll try to tell you why you died so suddenly, absurdly. You died because you forgot to look around you. You freed yourself too quickly and because you thought yourself free, you no longer wanted to look around you. You forgot about reality.

— You could have helped me, given me a sign.

— It's true that I believed you out of harm's way, safe from barking dogs. I imagined you passionate and as such able to repel bad fate. I believed you were stronger than reality.

— But imagining the scene, you could have changed its course. You could have made the bullet ricochet or wound me slightly.

— No. It was you or him. For if this man had only wounded you, you would have turned on him with such fury that you're the one who would have put him to death. One way or another, your life would have been ruined. Self-defense or not. That man, don't forget, had a fine reputation.

– You dare to tell me that in order to protect me from that man, that madman, you chose to get rid of me.

– I didn't kill you. That man killed you.

– But that man doesn't exist. You were under no obligation to make that man exist.

– That man exists. He could be compared to the invisible wire that sections reality from fiction. In getting closer to Mélanie you wanted to cross the threshold.

– I hold you responsible for his actions. For my death.

– I'm not responsible for reality.

– Reality is what we invent.

– Don't be cruel to me. You who are familiar with solitude, ecstasies and torments. You and I have never thought of protecting ourselves. In this we have come a long way but sooner or later reality catches up.

– I can reproach you for what is in your book.

– By what right?

– Reading you gives me every right.

– But as a translator you have none. You've chosen the difficult task of reading backwards in your language what in mine flows from source.

– But when I read you, I read you in your language.

– How can you understand me if you read me in one language and simultaneously transpose into another what cannot adequately find its place in it? How am I to believe for a single moment that the landscapes in you won't erase those in me?

– Because true landscapes loosen the tongue in us, flow over the edge of our thought-frame. They settle into us.

– I remember one day buying a geology book in which I found a letter. It was a love letter written by a woman and addressed to another woman. I used the letter as a bookmark. I would read it before reading and after reading. For me that letter was a landscape, an enigma entered with each reading. I would have liked to know this woman, I imagined the face of the woman for whom it was meant. It was during that time that I started writing the book you want to translate. Yes, you're right, there are true landscapes that pry us from the edge and force us onto the scene.

– I think there is always a first time, 'a first time when it must be acknowledged that words can reduce reality to its smallest unit: *matter of fact.*' Do you remember those words?

– No, but I think that whoever said that was right. I'm weary. Is there anything else you wish to know?

– I mostly wanted to hear you talk about death. But no matter what happens, we're alone, aren't we?

– Keep to beauty, have no fear. Muffle civilization's noises in you. Learn to bear the unbearable: the raw of all things.

DIMENSIONS

DESERT

Above all, hold the gaze. Empty, horizon or light, here the word *anatomy* is what sums up the appearance of things like an extended intuition of human presence, capable amid shapes of sustaining all comparisons. As though a slowing down of energy in the very place where it is limitless, perfect instantaneity of subjectivity. To face duration. Immobility like a grasping by reason in naked space. Irradiation of bodies, the time finally come to last.

Since I've been rereading this book I'm anchored at point zero, considering a thousand strategies and points of view which soon dissolve, abstraction, abstraction, the gaze melts. Yet the desert like a comment wrested from reality, an outgrowth of space capable of diverting all silences, of absorbing beauty, of engulfing reason into it, the desert progresses.

Need one counterfeit or resist what of the desert Laure Angstelle wanted to expose as a warning, an engaging circumstance? I am bound by her every proposal and yet I must from the desert extract all the scholia, the slightest sign of life, the light boldly in the gaze, this for mine own understanding.

If I let my thoughts run free, will it be possible for me to imagine the desert in the distance like a transection of fragility and endurance, to perfect this section until profiles emerge from it, evolving in the narrative, tamed like heat of a kind, an intensity punctuated by frights and ecstasies.

No, I am not at liberty to forget *Mauve Desert* even if my own equilibrium were at stake. I am in the midst of a partition in which I must all at once involve myself without conceit and answer for the images put forth by Laure Angstelle. Yet at the moment of writing these words it is the 'cluster of flowers' part that rushes like a torrent through my thoughts. Salt lakes that surge all in reflections, beauty's frosted surfaces.

Yes, here I am at the heart of wonderment, astray among minerals and fanatical beasts, having entered the arid and solar landscape stretching out, a discrete outline like laughter with multiple uses. Everything in me is inclined to the solitude that polarizes civilization and the real. For that which veils the gaze here works at restricting the bluff, the spectacle. No vertigo here. It is all about sojourning as if the body were preparing to last eternally, scoria, salt, skeletal structure, with no tragedy other than thirst and the trembling air that corrects the geometry of the great *saguaros,* their stubby arms like milestones in the distance. Here in the mauve I forget. I forget literature and civilization. I forget the smiles of the Renaissance and the ambiguity of the word passion, the heaviness of limbs, heads thrown back with ecstatic eyes, the pain and the powerful inclinations which re-member emotions. I forget danger. The turn of events. The danger there is in wanting to cheat reality. I lunge full-bodied into space knowing only too well that this cannot last for I am not at liberty to forget Mélanie, *her ways,* the movement of her thoughts, the speed that stones her, that opens up a passage for her onto everything it is permitted to imagine about despair, about violence, about anonymity and about color like a probable climate in vegetation.

What then is the desert? Could I insist for a long time on wanting to describe it, to desire it now lust for life, now uniform extinction of hope or lovely quietude?

To erase human traces, to fascinate with these same traces, derision, the approximate calculation of the life expectancy of a tin can, of a car wreck half-buried in sand, of a traffic sign at a crossroads. Of disappearance, traces, traces amassed. The exact calculation of languages that have ended up in space like an explosion.

Earth, dust, a landscape without windows, without shelter. Observed land of silence, preexistent beauty, the desert is indescribable.

DAWN

Dawn is what begins, distortion of night, strange coloring of feeling, a recorded version of light. One says glimmer, glimmer of hope and when this brushes against thinking, it is that the eyes are quite ready for the little flashes that refresh everyday life. Every morning dawn whitens the world of all its purplish noises.

Dawn is discrete. It quite naturally provides for the profile of things, outlines reality for us, prepares the spectacle while in our eyes the fade-ins – fade-outs follow in sequence till sunrise. Dawn exposes. Dawn, coloring matter which assigns to new beginnings. Dawn, latent heat.

'Yes, I have seen dawn. Often.' The dawn of the incense ceremony. Dawn in summer, dawn in winter. Dawn on exam days. Jet-lag dawn when thinking hallucinates, when memory coagulates like a substance foreign to the body and eyes slowly part their lashes upon all-architecture cities in the violated, baroque morning. And also the dawn that comes after night has ignited from a surplus of energy and suddenly life has started resembling slow music that licks the whole body and entrances it.

But does one really see dawn when night is left to seep into our lives to a point where the glimmer of day disintegrates in our eyes like a chilly tomorrow? Can one claim to have seen dawn when it is morning already and in the pallid cab bringing us home, the eye catches the long colorful shape of a transvestite, a junkie's crazed gaze, chapped hands, urine-stained pants? Does one see dawn when there is no more context and our senses grind emptiness calling for sleep, other artifices to enfold the body?

Dawn attracts, this is certain, dawn fascinates. She is at the edge of night, at the edge of the soul a quiet certitude, an appeasement of the eyes smitten with changes and utopias. One must be worthy of dawn.

Was that it, wanting dawn, that Mélanie had intuited when in the Red Arrow Motel the longing for dawn had violently made itself felt in her, a radical longing like a project of utter perdition or a will to total availability to all the mind's side-slippings. The need for dawn, desire to defy night, hour after hour building arguments, things sometimes enameled sometimes smooth sometimes kaleidoscopic opening onto multiple gardens or capable without warning of leading to euphoria. Wanting dawn meant making one's way through furtive intuitions which open only at night, meant hoping to know its secret whose meaning, having escaped from the light of day, could only rekindle its appeal. Or perhaps Mélanie had thought that a little perseverance would give her the energy to understand how time can, at night, become dislocated in the core of beings and cause their story to explode.

All of this I write down while trusting my instinct for I don't really know how to distinguish between Mélanie's 'taste for dawn' and Laure Angstelle's will to put an end to it all. Isn't there in what asserts dawn as 'a principle which exacerbates energy' a warning, an omen of violence, a projected *term*?

I cannot subscribe to 'the furor of dawn.' In my eyes dawn stands out like an image against a background of humility. A great calm, quiet certitude. Yes, quietude. A song composed of perfectly round mono-syllables which in the mouth are like clockwork, rondo, rose, a giration of color, which in the mouth are girasols, pebbles, precious stones, a outflow of fervor in time at the quiet hour when the dew settles all its smells on the jade foliage.

Dawn attracts. One can call it 'innocent' or cry while withdrawing this assertion; at dawn one can easily have the intention of disappearing, of slipping one's body into the underside of light, very softly.

LIGHT

Need one hold the gaze again, arrogantly allege that one is able to or imagine light as a wave encouraged by the heat on the skin, an intensity rendering bodies translucent, capable of filtering out the cold tight fists we raise to the sky? For in full light our whole body rears up, aura of being or fabulous animal, gifted with splendor and ingenuity.

Thus in the desert light works at dematerializing reality, leaving our gaze captive of what was, haunted by 'the definitive aspect of matter.' Light works without taking precautions and this is why when it dissolves the body we seek a center of gravity that no longer is. Acknowledge then that even in the middle of the desert vertigo can, threatening our verticality, force us to correct our equilibrium or to submit to an erratic fever on the ground gold-plated with reflections.

Light is tricky and as well harsh. Its progress can be observed upon skins but one can also lose the sense of reality when it traverses consciousness, brutal, unremitting, distancing points of reference and capable too of fixing them in eternity. Light subdues the gaze, dismisses the gaze, thanks it. No one escapes dismissal.

In the desert light bruises reality, shreds the fine fabric of colors every which way, suppresses shapes. We are unprotected against light for it is always when we are filled with wonder that light assails and abstracts from our gaze the infinitely precious relationship we entertain with reality. Thus at the very moment we believe ourselves in full possession of the real, there it goes exploding under our eyes, falling out on our shoulders, yoke of jade.

Light is harsh. How could I desert Mélanie? How to enter the angle of her gaze and spare myself the light? How to forget the instant? For therein lies the story of this book. The instant borne by a single symbol: light. Light crushing all perspective. Light spinning what is at stake. No book can be written without something being at stake. Life stakes, death stakes, I still don't know. But no book is written without stakes, brutal and immediate.

I'm writing all this while imagining the character and the auther picturing their existence like something attractive in life, a fluency of the body, a rhythm in the flesh, a carnival multiplying dawns, silks and bones in a costume blurred by light.

So it is! And also that unexpected image of light: there is the daughter and the mother, there are two heads of hair, in one a small silvery comb, its glimmering then upon reflection, the mirrored angles curve, rainbow, going from mother to daughter, silken strand, ancient tie reviving hair's suppleness, hair's strength. Precariousness of the image. Speed.

'Rapid light.' Where I stand light slants reality toward the cold side of winter. Light is a short interval keeping demons at bay. I tame at a distance. I am alongside. I take advantage of uncertainty, of the ambiguity I know I cannot escape: my cold sensitivity against the excessive sensitivity of Mélanie / Laure. Confrontation, validation. Question of *treatment*. Probable error, 'partial transcription of light deep in the mind.' The gaze melts. Light persists, blinding, sweeps away all intimacy, starts brushing dangerously close to time, to temples, again.

'I was leaning into my thoughts to make them slant reality toward the light.'

REALITY

Reality is what we recapture by an incalculable return of imaged things, like a familiar sense very distinctly set out in our lives. But to all of this there must be, we think, another sense, another version since we dream of it as we do of a musical accompaniment, a centered voice capable of securing for us a passage, a little opening. A voice which could, at equal distance from origins and death, activate the hypotheses, adapt the adornment, adjust the folds, the ornament, the anecdote ensuing from it like a work, regulate the alternating movement of fiction and truth.

Reality *counts for real*, therefore do we address ourselves 'little passion fire that pretexts' to what is most pressing in our biography and, is it a mistake, dictate to our voice extra syllables that make us lose sense, that undo the work undertaken by voice. But one takes the risk, one dives *quite naturally* into reality as if it were a valid category, an adequate landscape.

In full reality, we notice it unpretentiously as being all smells and food; a bit of fish, meat, fowl, a garlic bud, all of this spread out among the knives on the kitchen table. Strawberries, raspberries scattered, little motifs in the apron's color scheme. Fridays of emotion, cool drinks, flowers in a large vase. Reality is on time, full of topicality, calendar, nice photographs, December a dog, January a goat, May a butterfly. Sometimes all year round, naked girls spread out between Sunday and the end of the month. Reality models the body, tightens around the neck, the waist, cuts beautiful shapes into the white, blue, pink and black; an old custom the costume. Reality scrolls by linear,

skirts fates, mates males and females in great metaphoric beds. Reality
wends its way, enumerates the names of cities, of entire families, lists
the dead, states beautiful days, the season, incidents. Crashes. Starts
over, hunger again, thirst again, a gregarious grey morning again.
Unpretentiously, reality walks around Geiger counter in hand. Reality
counts!

'Some day I will exit reality,' find a lode, a *vein,* the little opening in
which I will be *forced to slow down,* to reduce the intensity, the speed of
the image. Redo everything, body, weight and volume, the length of
winter, nature and representation, framework of the spirit.

Until then I must give meaning to everything by which I exist.
Mauve Desert is an accident. Nothing tragic but like all things that
cause surprise, that work toward modifying the familiar setting, the
cold habit, this book assigns me other tasks. For example, *isolating
reality,* yes, soundproofing it like a room where I could involve myself
in the most concrete adventures of the spirit in the company of Laure
Angstelle and her characters. No familiar noise would filter in to mislead my perception. Certainly the objects would be the same: the
bookshelves, a large poster of the flowering Sonora, my three cacti, the
bed, the television set, the ashtray, the frosted window, but none of this
could distract me to the point of awakening in me some memory.
Reality would be condensed to the maximum. I would be able to feel it
on my skin, follow perfectly the conversation between Mélanie and
her mother, hear everything the television announcer is saying. Reality
would be quite palpable, concrete, dense. Colors would be precise,
words useful, univocal. I would observe Lorna, her walk, her muscled
arms, a smile, I think. Emboldened by the presence of women, I would
even go so far as to talking a bit about what is going on in my life, how I
prepare my classes, the beauty of autumn, summer's white afternoons,
tennis, my partners, my opponents, my lost balls. My restlessness
would be great.

Be this as it may, we who would like to isolate reality from fiction,
we who would like it to count for real, here we are, by an incalculable
return of imaged things, once again among familiar noises, at equal
distance between chance and finality.

BEAUTY

A faltering, a drop in tonality, a break in rhythm, one can think beauty as akin to signs drawn admirably to surprise us. Beauty inevitably curves the breath, harmonizes emptiness, *suddenly* fragrances succeed one another, the pupil, we will see, dilates, the eyelids close anyway. Beauty as though it were no longer about living. The precious moment. Frosted surface. Impassioned consciousness.

One can imagine too that unconditional responsiveness we have when faced with likelihood, that sustained appearance of the will to be, in spite of the cold, in spite of it all, beauty, for we sometimes think this, that beauty borders on the most unpleasant sensations, borders on the roughest ways of living and speaking.

Beauty, I know not how to say, and yet, said she, 'beauty encroaches upon beings.' I know not how to translate this intention, perhaps of happiness, perhaps of nostalgia or of some other sentiment which could, at a given point in life, blend so closely with joy that as such it is termed a taste of eternity.

In the exploded distance, beauty moves, impossible figure of fondling. Fragrant labella.

'Beauty is before reality,' of a polysemic, unthinkable antecedence, too pacific for our eyes abridged in the distance, unable afar to think without seams, fragment, history, difference. The body of women tossed about in the distance, history, difference. Beauty precedes desire, its fragment, history, the transection of reality and fiction. Beauty *fata* of memory.

'Beauty is before reality.' Is it really possible to think of beauty as

preceeding all reality, *paradise lost,* without risking the obliged transection of sentences and inflection of the voice, without succumbing to
the definite attraction of nostalgia crossed with fervor: a sustained
prayer. Man, it is a known fact, is acquainted with prayer, prayer is his
elevation but could it be that, through other paths and passions of the
soul, Mélanie has *achieved* in all innocence and intuition the same resonance of being? Need one think that any radical intuition of beauty
sends thinking back to that tight fist of imagination kneeling, proud
with instinct? Need one think that this is a routine imposed upon
whomever leans violently on the side of light? Need one take the risk of
pride exploding, winter's cold beauty, 'it is snowing in the everlasting'?

Cold beauty of the eternal, beauty intimidates, I mean it threatens
supremely like a masked language. For that which takes shape in the
warm belly of the species transforms itself, language, break, shimmer-
ing, seduction: beauty, angle of reflection, selective neuron, source
tongue.

It happens too that on occasion one may think that beauty has no
use for the gaze, that it reduces comparisons to nothing, makes sover-
eign bodies breathless, for beauty cannot be approached with an
instrument, even were it our gaze at its extreme precision point.
Beauty thwarts motives, the lust for life, awaits the hollow moment
where endlessly the life equation surprises, levels out at the end of the
assertion the extended loop of the letter.

One may think whatever one likes, beauty puts an end to intimacy in
us, yes, threatens supremely like a cold language. Seamlessly, without
interrupting the smile, without denouement. Beauty proceeds.

FEAR

Fear is a reality that clutters fiction for without it we would juggle with our lives much beyond the lessons learned.

Fear mobilizes hopes and energy, in whose name, in the name of what? They will say fear is individual, they will say terror is collective, they will say precisely the opposite, fear remains a shape smashing against the window. Wounded, fear strikes, cocked, fear strikes dread. Fear is for every woman a signal to withdraw. It is not her limit, it is in her head a 'hollow' manner of vigilance forming between subjectivity and reality: a pocket of water in the gaze which makes the world blur, quick take. Fear impedes.

They will say that 'too great a sensitivity' moors fear to the body and that any expertise then becomes impossible, only bewilders consciousness as if *the images,* O manifest multitude, astounding installations, were suddenly going to take a graft from our self.

Fear rewinds catastrophes, in the lower belly, the contortion. Also can be seen the face's slackening: the grimace, the antics absorbed by the restless limbs, it spies. Behind the television screen the beast sniffs smells of good cooking and flesh. The beast is elusive, night, metal, mask, 'fear gleams in the petrified forest.' This is when they say that a wind of panic is blowing on the whole region, at its heart and the body exhausts itself quite completely, falls breathless, breath and sweat intermingled. It's nothing! Perhaps is there nothing but a rate of growth, a burst of laughter, a nerve suddenly, too great a sensitivity. A twisting of the features which accelerates the passing of time upon faces.

'My mother was talking about fear. A slow fear, a livid fear' as if fear were capable of maneuvers among the body's fluids, as if from fear could be born strange sensations, skilled in the pit of the belly at igniting feeling, at stoking excitement. This fear is unknown by most. It is a fear sometimes heard about and which, it is said, makes women attentive to the surprising sounds their voice can produce when they are seeking in the same breath to repress the slow fear and the definite attraction which, like a ludic and poignant impropriety, pass through them though they are without words to comprehend. It is an incongruous fear seen mostly in the islands, when islands begin to take shape within us like a hope we must learn to distinguish.

But other fears, other words: 'the heavy fear.' Is it lapse of fervor or that which constricts the senses, their distribution over the skin ever ready for more, the folds one would wish open, lips speaking without anyone being able to feel sorry for civilization? The fear there is in writing as if the real were going to find itself reinforced, *enlivened* by the repartee, which secretly animates the beautiful breath of living, which unveiled would in the distortion of accomplished meaning go and take place next to the sharp objects we use in the daily task of living. Fear is strange. It is akin to the objects we take in our hands, some not as ugly as others, less opaque, lighter. Then fear glides over our skin, cools the palm, momentarily creates the impression that the fallen creatures in our gaze will at last be able to withdraw without our features being submitted to torsion. Freely until: *raptus.*

Fear, they will say is like shame, quite useless. They will say 'it doesn't matter when you accelerate' believing it is enough to conceal behind the screen the deranged signs of desire, to refer threat to the bottom of the screen, *simulation.* A little snow will be seen. They will believe it is enough, in the fervor of the night, to reestablish *speaking.* But fear, let there be no secret about it, is as widespread as men's speeches.

CIVILIZATION

There is a time of believing where we refine the natural gestures that bring us closer to the image, others that throw us back into discourse and haste. This time of believing is a time of civilization, a certitude of beings that fills chance with architectures and voice explosions. 'The inexperience of dying'* is for any civilization a form of *eagerness*. An engaging spontaneity capable of calculations which, without further warning than hallucinated metaphor, repress nature in us. But nature is said to be everywhere for inside our skull, it exaggerates, embroiders, bluffs, amasses seas, canyons, forests and deserts, sumptuous dawns, orchids with no name. Nature dismisses us. So we occupy ourselves with the answer, seeking in language the tools liable to divert us from the nostalgia endlessly at work among the most extravagant settings. Yet civilization is always very simple: a woman, a birth, machinery, death. *The trick.* 'Mothers are as fragile as civilization,' she says.

There is also a time of believing which absorbs all panics, that time is called *time of vegetation* or, if one prefers, *time of animation,* a semantic counterpart to what languishes, at the limit, one could speak of a *crystallization* of the machinery, exactly as if one wanted to signify a hard transparency and a very brief time span, *suddenly,* between attraction and repulsion, an indifference which surprises us.

When at rest, we like to think that civilization is a sandglass, a clock, a quartz capable of telling us time, a coaster protecting against the habit of dark circles. As a hobby, we are dog-loving and trigger-happy. We quite like demography and sometimes a few sighs. When at rest, civilization inclines to the image, to certain mockeries conducive to the denouement, when night has fallen, of some fictions. We then dream about our gestures as though they could dissuade us from death.

In theory, civilization is a model valid for many conquests and conversions. Charged letter, it accomplishes wonders, designs beautiful destinies. This is, they say, its surface of influence, its *manner.*

But where I stand, mated with Mélanie's voice, humanity and civilization form two words, a blunder, a semantic shift, a discrepancy that wounds, a hewing of the horizon which sends back versions, the slope of the gaze in the topsy-turvy things of desire and of dawn. Where I now find myself, snow again, garden-side, sonorous rain like a transposition of the effect, rain makes my body submit, my thoughts focused on the horizon.

Where I now find myself, it is possible to hone hope among the dense lightrays.

* Maurice Blanchot.

A BOOK TO TRANSLATE

(continued)

For over a year now Maude Laures had been preparing *her manuscript*. This morning the sky was blue. Two or three clouds, little breaks in the distance. Maude Laures opened the refrigerator, poured herself a Coke. Then she felt like leaving, like taking the road to Québec City. The river would be beautiful and wide under the harsh light of March.

Maude Laures went back to her work table, took the book, removed the elastic band holding the pages together. All the pages were annotated, here *polysemy* blue, *sound track* green, *must check* red, *incomprehensible* black, *familiar* yellow, *which gender?* pink, *what verb tense?* mauve. In the margins 'cautions' that could be mistaken for comments entered in pencil. Sometimes a drawing to facilitate representation.

at the bottom of the page ELIMINATE ALL THE *like(s)* IF POSSIBLE.

Maude Laures put her lenses in, got ready in front of the mirror. She suddenly had the feeling she was soon going to be nothing but a resonance instrument. She saw herself by turns lyre, theorbo, viola. The mauve decomposed, was recomposed, palimpsest, in her eyes, an air.

She opened the drawer, took out a white shirt, got dressed, looked at a bit of reality through the window, confused to revolt and revolver in her head, went back to the mirror, put on some lipstick, then went and sat in front of the silent television set. Lit a little cigar.

The bed was cozy. She woke up at noon, furious at herself as if she had been a black drizzle in the light. The poster of the Sonora was in bloom, the file folders pell-mell on the table. Newspaper clippings. File cards and definitions like as many deflagrations in consent. Maude Laures got up, parted the curtains. The glittering day entered her head. She leaned over, picked up an envelope, thought that the horizon was like a great female nude very tempting for the eyes. Then she started over again as she did every day, hunched over her table, her eye stern, her hand tensed toward the words that could be rescued from the desert, patrolling Laure Angstelle's imaginary space. She thought 'this comes close to emptiness,' was afraid for a moment then refocused her thinking on 'cartridges and all weapons.'

'When two words are identical, you must not take undue offence or think you have been wronged in terms of choice. Simplicity is a fine patience of meaning.' Maude Laures sometimes felt the need to repeat a few recommendations out loud to herself. It even happened that she would interrupt her work and, arms flailing, indulge in long oratorical jousts in the middle of her room. Words flew high, words flew low, she caught them, cast them out, recast them. Her game was a beauty, taste buds aflame. The dictionary, well too bad! Lingua of fire, long-spoken. Lai.

Words were in the mouth like little pits 'the hardest and brightest part,' a presence, a solid body needing to be expelled after a while by bringing the tongue forward as if preparing to grimace, then in one breath, projecting in front of oneself the indivisible part. Between the teeth then remained only flesh and taste, edible part, a good daily portion. But a whole word too could be spit out.

Maude Laures would have liked to take off for Québec City. Get out on the road a bit for she thought that the highway's repeating image could be of use along the temples for some comparisons, compensate her inexperience of speed and of raving. For here, she thought, here, there is nothing to fire the imagination. Imagination is wholly devoted to extricating us from doubt and cold. But Maude Laures persisted, she could see herself at the wheel, screwing up her eyes as fences, shacks and silos rising up from the melting snow and the mud shone at last in the distance like similes, little disks reminding her of skilful children's gestures on the surface of the river making stones ricochet.

Also that day, she worked well into the night on the word *ricochet*. To ricochet was in effect a word that could save many a situation: 'her gaze and her thinking ricocheted, the bullet ricocheted and missed her, the ball ricocheted on a chair, went astray and got lost in the television set, the light ricocheted on the bumper, the conversation ricocheted on a word.'

There was no more space in the margin so Maude Laures started ticking off other words that could in her language get meaning restarted and spare her from facing Angela Parkins' brutal end.

One more dawn. Spring was to be expected. Light encroached more and more on reality as though it were a question of giving it a comprehensive meaning or of exposing matter as a novelty when the time has come to adapt and that bodies suggest refined tastes, treading with silken step, beauteous slowed motion of the image, in search of some universals.

Trajectory, thought Maude Laures, trajectory. And she progressively got accustomed to the idea of becoming a voice both other and alike in the world derived from Laure Angstelle. The characters would soon slip away one after the other, become little transparencies in the distance, crystallize. She would be alone in her language. Then would come substitution.

The time had come for taking on the book body to body. A time that would give way to astonishment regarding things only very seldom seen, sited in the background of our thoughts. From one tongue to the other there would be meaning, fair distribution, contour and self-encounter, that moving substance which, it is said, enters into the composition of languages and makes them tasteful or hateful. Maude Laures knew that now was the time to slip anonymous and whole between the pages.

Full desert, full horizon. In the lower belly, there where the tongue wants, a fine slow fear was beginning to well up, to distribute tasks.

It was now spring. The light was dazzling and one could once again claim that words would, in moving from the *innocent* book to the translated book, play out their part, sweeping Maude Laures away in the flow of constraints, exceptions and principles. Now it would be necessary, in the un-said, to play a close game.

Where characters, objects, fear and desire had been, words were all Maude Laures could see now. Words were taking over the action, poised for the capture of senses.

MAUVE
THE
HORIZON

LAURE ANGSTELLE

Translated by Maude Laures

A N G L E   P R E S S

The desert is indescribable. Light swallows everything, harsh gulf. The gaze melts. Yet, today. Very young, I was already despairing about humanity. Every new year's day I could see it dispersing in hope and in excess. Very young, I would take off in my mother's car and head for the desert where I was obstinate in front of the day, the night and at dawn, about wanting everything. I was weaving the light. I was driving fast and also slowly; I was following the little fragments of life aligned in my gaze, mauve horizon.

Skilful I was in the game of discernment but inside me was a desire such that, without obstacle, it anguished me like an overabundance of energy. Then would come the pink, the red and the grey among the stones the mauve and the slow dawn. In the distance the glare of a tourist helicopter.

Very young, there was no future and the world resembled a burned-out house like the one at the corner of the street torched by 'strangers,' so said my mother who had served them a drink. My mother thought only one of them was armed but no concern came over her for all the others had blue eyes. My mother often said that men were free to act as in books. She would finish her sentence then, once the uneasiness had passed, sit in front of the television set. I would watch her profile and in my gaze the hairpin she always wore stood out like a silk thread. Her apron was yellow with lovely flowers. My mother never wore dresses.

I was driving through the night, wild with arrogance. I was 15 years old. This was exquisite like great power, a gentle way of getting lost in the dark and a thousand delirious scenes in the vicinity of the eyes.

I knew the desert well, its little paths and the high roads in the distance. Lorna, beloved friend of my mother's had taught me to give meaning to the images trembling in the stone and in dust. She spent long moments telling me stories full of landscapes, exotic types of vegetation, talked to me about remote lands which could not be compared to the soil of my birth. Lorna was storytelling. I figured that somewhere inside her a strange passion was compelling her to invent animal names, to dream of impossible colors, to fake the shape of reptiles. I knew this for I was well able to distinguish the rattlesnake from the coral, eagles from piscivorous species. Lorna was lying. Lorna dared to say so many things. Her words were so hard and unreal that I sometimes had the impression of a howling when they came flaming across the threshold of her mouth.

Lorna had not known childhood, only some girls from her class with whom she got together at recess. The girls loved her. She loved kissing them on the mouth when school got out.

The first time I saw Lorna I found her pretty and said a dirty word. I was 5 years old. During the meal my mother was smiling. They were looking at each other and whenever they opened their mouths there was an emotion. I watched them closely, their lips especially, as if they were a pronounced surface of the face, a swelling animating the conversation right into their eyes. Lorna marveled over the moss on the mountaintops, soft against the shins. My glass of milk spilled over on the tablecloth which suddenly resembled a large map with a river that flowed onto my knees. My mother mopped everything up, made a game of it.

I often took my mother's car. Long before I was allowed everything. Under the sun, at twilight and even at night, I would leave in spite of the worried words cried out by my mother which would land in the parking lot dust. I have always searched for the desert, for very young I wanted to know everything about beauty, about light, to distance fear and death. I knew my mother would experience a great sense of loss but to the reflections of magic in her smooth hair I preferred the sun's burning reflection, night in the eyes of hares like a grasping of life, to dazzle myself. 'Violence and aridity be mine' and I would accelerate, wild with the damned energy rushing to my head. Some day I would be *fata de fata*, edge on edge, some day at dawn I would be insensitive to everything, equations and humanity, its unreason erupted at the back of madmen's forlorn gaze. I was driving fast, cut off from history, torrid silence. Repeating 'so many times I have ended up in utopia.'

At night the desert was beauty, reflection of vivid beasts, ephemeral, silence, *senitas*. Under the Meteor's headlights humanity was a misleading deposit. Humanity was fragile without Arizona. *So fragile.* I was 15 and my voice was shaking, impatient and breakable. I wanted for my whole body to be necessary. I drove well. I was capable of aligning night in me, of threading my way through shadows. I could foresee everything and this temporarily relieved me of clutter and of words. Eternity was in my brain like a shadow, dark aspect of desire, a music making me sink into the tracings of highways. Humanity was fragile, suspended like a universe over cities, explosive. Everything was fragile, I knew it, I had always thought so. At 15, I claimed that everything would be great. Like my mother, I believed that everything was a game of pretend.

Shadows in passing swallow hope. There are no shadows at night, when the sun is at its zenith. Everything is *matter* of fact and reality chills us to the bone. But reality is confinement, a little grave that misleads desire. Reality is a flash-fire that pretends. I was 15 and with my entire being I was leaning on the fragile side of my thoughts to make them penchant of the moment, to make reality count for real.

Now follow the directions, the arrow pointing toward the Red Motel. Park the car. Sweat. The Bar. The bar's polished surface resembles a screen: women and men are talking and in the setting repeating themselves like shadows on the wall. They look like stains. I down my beer and life goes on in the brouhaha*.

---

* Expressive form of the verb to exist, can, depending on context, be pejorative or meliorative.

1

O'blongman puts his briefcase on the bed. It is hot in the room. He loosens his shirt collar. He heads for the bathroom. He thinks about the explosion. He imagines it and it is not enough for him. What! He remembers beautiful footpaths, autumn in full color. He looks at himself in the mirror. He dries his hands. He thinks about the explosion, he thinks about it and there is emptiness in his head. He puts his jacket on a chair. A pencil falls from a pocket. He does not pick it up. He lights a cigarette. He feels the brim of his felt hat. He thinks about the explosion. He caresses round words which in his mouth form Sanskrit sentences, words that enchant, he knows it. He paces the room. The smoke from his cigarette curls a little cloud over his head. O'blongman knows the value of words. He thinks about the explosion. A single mathematical error could alter the course of history. O'blongman stretches out on the bed. Images, then from white to orange the earth turns jade. – *Death / I / am / death* – I'm a sonofabitch. O'blongman falls asleep, a little grave calculated like an explosive shape in his body.

I was capable of surprising my mother. She was capable of throwing me off track. She had great power for splintering my gaze. When I would see her so close to Lorna and that between them was just enough distance for me to imagine in their bodies an excitation, images rushed through me, nape of the neck, nakedness, blissful shoulders.

I'm moving forward. My gaping mouth swallowing rock songs, all the rhythm, howling lyrics and speed. They interrupt the music. A man's voice announces a disaster, an earthquake. I lean on the voice and it gets lost inaudible *tsunami* in the distant Pacific. I don't like my mother to be alone at night. It haunts me. Mothers are like civilization, fragile in front of their television sets, forgotten like some ancient knowledge. Mothers are open spaces. I love driving violently fast in the Meteor. I love the repeated horizon. No fear, no panic comes my way in the middle of the night or during cloud of sand and I can't see a thing in front of me. I stop, I become living matter; isolated from everything, hands on the steering wheel, sunkdeep into the gloom, I listen to the world's fracas burying my car in sand. I submit, blinded. I look into the inside at my brain moving forward in time, multiplying seconds, crystals, aerial creatures in the fold of the eyelids. I follow trails, the trace of time, triangles, spirals, around ruins, barkhans, mobiles. Only once, only once, did I see words I was unable to read. And the signs scattered at once as though at the back of the mind the body of the letter could not withstand light, such a presence.

I was driving ravenous. Exposing myself to every risk so that consciousness could rise up, violent and ongoing in the heart of the night and the desert. I was 15, with all of time and the horizon ahead of me. In my mother's white shell I was speed, civilization, in the distance, city, lost gaze, ruin in reverse. I was moving forward, exemplary in my solitude, with at my feet a brake to prevent disasters. There is no need amid snakes and cacti to despair, for night is always raving blue.

I look like my mother when humanity in distress looms in the distance and with a great laugh makes one go pale. My mother never cried. I never saw her give in to such disorder. No doubt was she unable to reflect on solitude with exactness. And yet my mother trembled when the noise of beings assailed her but remained insensitive to the cold and mysterious thing that is solitude. In the most difficult moments she would declare: 'This is a male, rest is required, this is a woman, meaning is required.' My mother was austere like a man used to nature and danger. She did not like men but fiercely defended the feelings liable to toughen the over-fertile pulp of her imagination. She was a woman whose expressionless voice could echo and suddenly cause reason to worry, mislead judgment.

Every time I think of my mother, I imagine girls in swimsuits stretched out, long nostalgic bodies by the Motel pool. This motel, my mother had rebuilt it over the years then kept it going with care, gestures and courteous smiles despite the heat of Tucson afternoons. But everything is vague. Before Lorna's arrival there is only a busy space filled with customers, salesmen, the continuous hum of the vacuum-cleaner.

Lorna, this novel presence, will always be in my memory like a point of reference among school sessions where writing and reading take shape like an acquiring of knowing. I read a lot but, strange coincidence, always in Lorna's presence. She spied on me. On the alert and silent, Lorna searched my face for the signs which in me produced images. As soon as I looked up, her gaze would mist over as though the words she imagined in my mouth could, in her presence, transform themselves or be shared like an emotion. Then, to divert her attention and especially to keep her from reading my mind, I would talk about eating.

One day when I wanted blank sheets of paper and in a rush went looking for my mother, I fell upon the knotted shape of a double presence. My mother was sitting on Lorna's lap and Lorna was absent-mindedly scribbling huge letters on her back. I asked for some paper and Lorna answered that writing served no purpose, that playing hard and screaming loud were more useful. I was about to protest, to say that every letter was a game, a bird, a cat, a fl... when I noticed that one of the flowers of my mother's apron was entirely covered by Lorna's free hand.

Yet that night. Very young I learned to love the storm, the fire, the lightning, the electric lines that scratch the horizon as if every tear were going to open a passage to thinking. On dry storm nights I would explode in the distance, clench my jaw, shaking, my whole body charged with tears and mental cold. Then I would surrender to all the flashes of lightning as though it were a matter for the flesh of being momentarily linked to the noise neurons make when faced with immensity. Then the body, abridged like a certitude. The desert drinks everything in. Furor and solitude.

In the desert one must want to continue one's way, to enter the world's gaping. A few clouds here and there brush against the horizon, draw little pellets in the air. I know the permanent flash of metal, small shots, dust-shots, lead shots. I know what is necessary, daughter of the desert, I have never stopped crossing swords and sentiments.

2

O'blongman is watching. He stretched out fully clothed. He is replaying the explosion. His clothes are wrinkled, the shoes are dirty. He muses a moment on art and on the beauty of the solar spectrum, then he gets up and goes to the dresser. The small magazine of naked women is in its place, stashed away under the white, orange and jade file folders. He takes the magazine, goes back to the bed, plumps up the pillow, makes himself comfortable. He leafs through, stops here, there, he is waiting for something to happen. 'Now we are all dogs.' O'blongman reviews the sex parts. No faces, no faces especially! The genitals make dark circles around the labiate images. Then the circles explode. He closes his eyes. It is gently snowing like during that beautiful winter at Princeton, the eve of his 20th birthday. Once again insomnia. The confusion between the mathematical calculations and the results. O'blongman knows large blue lakes, thinks of the forest, of amethyst trees forever petrified. It is snowing in the everlasting. Splendor and splendor. 'Now that death and writing are on the tongue a strict prohibition.' O'blongman hears the explosion. His whole body tenses, stiff shape. His felt hat has fallen, limp. He lights a cigarette.

In the desert fear is exact, well-proportioned, wears no mask. It is useful, precise, does a good job. Fear, here, is frequented like a natural history. It is exceptionally succinct, a few illustrations: beaks, fangs, stingers, forked tongue.

At the Motel though, fear frightens. On the screen as in thought, it fragments bodies, assassinates daily. Fear sniffs boredom and sends chills down the back. Fear insists, amplifies the torment of living, permutates certitudes and farfetched stories in the brain.

I was 15 and I'm talking about fear still for it always takes me by surprise. But exact fear is beautiful. Every night it can be seen wandering, strong remnant of eternity in the petrified forest. Yes, exact fear kindles the plexus and plaits strange suns in the eyes.

When Lorna came to live with us, my mother hesitated to talk about fear. I felt her, confused, slow and at the same time ready to declare herself. My mother would say: 'Lorna, I'm at my wit's end, I sense a danger' and Lorna in her laughter, in her gestures, in her eyes, embodied an imprecise threat which would break my mother's voice. Whenever Lorna dove into the pool with her whole winged body, my mother would plead: 'Lor, Lor, don't do that' and Lorna, amused by the incongruous fear seizing my mother, would take me in her arms and we would become dolphins, grey backs, big white horses cresting on the sea. My mother would lean over the water and I could see her body like a giant shape cut out against the sky. And then with a mouth full of bubbles and babbling with joy I would resurface; eyes red with chlorine, I would spit supremely on the world like a great dragon.

I will perhaps talk about all that some day, my life. Some day when nothing seems true to me anymore. It's already saying a lot when I talk about the night and the desert for inside me the immediate horizon hones the biographical edge. I have abused everything, the stars, the dawn, touched stone, known metal, caressed the sleepy shape of beasts, maneuvered so many times in view of the magical horizon to make the energy haunting me unfurl like an answer, some audible thing amid the noise, instinct. I was 15 and I knew how to choose between people, the double, the character. I knew *fata de fata* that a touch of fear was, by night, synonymous with enfranchisement. I was pressing on the accelerator and fear, oh night, noise, so fragile a body when silence does not let up in the dark.

Night! Yes, I have seen dawn. Often. Dawn, the specters, the fascinating spectacle of time as whirlwind, dust. I was speeding along. I was howling in full light of day. At night on the highway, I lived hard. Then once again there was the pool, girls in swimsuits and my mother on the phone all involved in her voice, fully clothed in her image. Lorna would come near her and my mother would decide on the moment, on the caress. In their eyes dailiness was suddenly true, without a screen, then detected by my gaze, would suspend itself like a decision.

Some nights the gloom would dry words up and it fascinated me to see the skin of delirium drop like fever at dawn. Then I could exist without compare, capable only of great thirst between my lips and the high wind. Desiccation.

I was always certain of everything. Of gestures, of the weather, of distance, of the horizon. Of everything except words. The slow fear of words. A frightful pain in all my veins.

One day in May when the heat was still stirring very strongly in the atmosphere, I stopped right in the middle of nowhere to examine a huge *saguaro* between life and death. As usual I was singing – over and over, oh to get away. Then as though the horizon had suddenly turned to me, I felt the heavy fear coming over me. The *saguaro* was wavering. Words. Everything was in slow motion, life like an unreal synthesis achieved in the body. But no more road, no more cactus, no dawn at all, only the survival instinct which with one hard blow returns words to their true value.

'Paper!' I went back to the car, opened the glove compartment, moved the revolver, grabbed the little notebook to write all of this or about that, I madly felt like doing it. It was exploding in my head, *beauty was going gently by like a shadow, skirting the great canyons, snaking, arroyo, agony, cumulate, somersault, hurtling among the organ pipes, the teddy bears, the thorns and the flowers, it excited me, it went wild, brave beast, consenting epidermis,* multi-layered life. Then fear went and paled in the distance.

The horizon is curving. The atmosphere satiny around the car. I head back to the Motel. I drive fast, in mind, my mother and Lorna. My mother is distant, Lorna, in front of the television set. Crazy, crazy disappointment, crazy gleam in my room, quick my fingers there, that's it, wet, waver, get m *'off.*

That night words whirled for a long time in my head, wrapped round me, got emotion spinning around. I had the impression of a thousand loops in my body, solemn intuitions about life, concerning death. Then reality became an IMAGE. I fell asleep at dawn, swaddled, siren, object of the image.

Now, I know delayed-action fear. I spend all my time in front of the television set. I edge around the harsh noise of voices, the anxiety that communicates itself. I know reality. Humanity like a shadowed shape. It moves slowly, ophidian, skin of slowness in the dust, camouflage, slough. Motionless, dead skin, little fetish just above ground level, asleep at the foot of *senitas* and *ocotillos.* The fear of skin hollows the back of the eyes while orange and jade in the distance form lovely footpaths in the leafage. Skin frightens the ignorant. That's skin.

That same month my mother was sad and Lorna gentle with me. I pestered my mother so she would look at what I had written. I would leave messages everywhere like so many clues to my desire. At night my mother would tell Lorna my story but leave out the narrative. Lorna would laugh nervously. So I would turn up the volume and the whole of panic fear would take place in reality like a dirty eye.

Ever since I had dared to write, reality was settling into every thing, taking up a lot of space. Customers were arriving, Texans, 'pale birds' from Wisconsin and Minnesota. Lots of old ladies and gents. Salesmen. Sometimes some women who when they were together created a brouhaha. More young girls in swimsuits. I listened to the conversations in the Bar. People based what they said on clichés, others laughed coarsely; it seemed to me that all were paying dearly for the scant power of living.

One evening I finally saw the famous Angela Parkins whom my mother said was excessive. She was still young. They said she was a geometrist. She would come to the Bar once a month. She would have discussions with men. I listened to their conversation. I couldn't understand everything and when that was so, I studied their physiognomies. I would accumulate my thoughts then all of a sudden relax the masks and the smiles. Only Angela Parkins' rare face continued to live inside me like an intimate thing.

The evening went on slow and smooth when Angela Parkins' voice detonated like some device at first unusual, then threatening. Then the voice rose hysterical and caprizant, burst in on me wild. My mother says it was the alcohol, too much alcohol, but I could clearly see that in Angela Parkins' voice there was more than mere debauchery. Infinitely more than intoxication. She was all at once island of resistance, witness-mound in the distance of the desert. The evening continued to be smoky. Angela Parkins retired before 11 o'clock. I followed her to the parking lot. I was 15 and wanted my whole body to be necessary. Reality had a meaning. How?

The next day I left for Albuquerque where my cousin Grazie lived.

3

The man's eyes were insanely arrogant. He was nodding his head and with every movement there was the explosion. The ceiling, the floor, the explosion. His whole body was subjected to acceleration. His image was stretching, impossible sum, fantastic mass. He was lost, no more body in him, just the dust falling out all over like cold reason. He would never recover from winter, even though he knew how to be so warm-hearted when the smell of dew helped him hope again. O'blongman felt terrorized. Shadows were multiplying, aberrant and untouchable. He dreamed of poems and of Sanskrit but already ashes, already blood were entering the open and silent mouth which in his mind obstructed the beautiful image in a thousand crystals he had invented. Then o'blongman drew figures on the wall. Compulsively drew death. His body spent itself against the wall. His shadow. The explosion was perfect in jade.

I was driving calmly. It was torrid, luminous. No music, no voice. Only me. Silence everywhere. I had chosen to impose full sunlight on myself, to exhaust my body as if this could help me recapture the time from before reality. I was driving and the desert was now a real danger, dry and cutting, full of traps. I hadn't brought a single drop of water. I forced heat, thirst, torments upon myself in order that the small real things one sees along highways find their resolution in me. In my civilized body I wanted the beast to sum up its code, that in the hyperreality of blue, images be reduced to a few glimpses, that the violent flow of words cease. Only what's body. Nothing to think. Heat, asphalt.

I sum up reality, my life in the blinding light. One day I dreamed full feeling between Phoenix and the petrified forest. In the space *everything was ablaze, carnival voice the horizon, beautiful masked ball, cavalcade, the forest ferns in a fury, fiery beauty, there were so many words yet as long as thinking practice patience.*

I had now entered the fear of the unspeakable. Involuntarily, I had gone over the limit, fractured fright and now everything was offset. A huge fold in silence. In the desert one gives in without calculating. Faced with the horizon, the body exposes itself, avid, to finding no sense.

I was now driving all a-glee imagining Grazie to whom I would talk about Angela Parkins, about this woman met in the rain of a Tuesday's night. I would shiver. I would make up stories. I would tell with tongue afire, everything I had felt as in a dream in the petrified forest. I would dare say so many things. Grazie would encourage me. 'One more story, another version, your true face. Talk, tell me everything. Tell too about Lorna and your mother. Their laughter, their fear, their voices, the night, their words. Talk to me, be flame, lick, light up so that mauve will awaken in us wide-ranging ways of dreaming. Ignite in me that which, perhaps, some day.'

Grazie was older than me by 2 months. We were, according to our mothers, like 'real sisters.' My mother had told me everything. 'It happened one beautiful April night. We were both pregnant, round, if only you could have seen us, rounded and velvety, ripe, just right like syllables, echoing atop Dante's View. If only, Mélanie, you had seen us, but the night.'

I'm driving slowly toward Albuquerque. O certitude! Grazie is expecting me. At the junction of (10) and (15), a gang of bikers are smoking with their noses in the air. Two girls are talking, a bottle of beer in hand. One of them flashes me a victory sign and the other one, barely set back in the spatial plane, violently 'up-yours' me with her middle finger, then the whole fist up. I accelerate. I know reality. Fear is nothing, it's nothing when one is fast so fast. Fear faints dark spot in the rearview mirror.

The road was like a time warp imperceptible in the trembling air. I was 15 with in front of me all of reality to ruin my existence. Like that freedom which, where I grew up, was a weapon capable of keeping fear and nostalgia at bay. There was also another freedom, lighter that one, which smelled clean, incense and powder. And then freedom all of a sudden BANG would aim at freedom. Give me a bite of freedom, said the men. Give me a bit, replied the women. Ah, freedom, how it led people astray!

I lost the desert. I lost the desert in the night of writing. There no doubt comes a moment when one has to know to stop, to halt in front of stupidity, to acknowledge that words are not always worthy or that they can cloud our enthusiasm, outwit our fine thinking maneuvers. Now, *matter* of fact must bring the desert back to life in me so that once again coral snakes and rufous bobcats can brush the ground with their colors. Antelope jackrabbits must again regain their speed, their white coat, the mystery stones walking Death Valley once again mark the horizon with their weight. *Matter* of fact must return, certitude must like an overload of images at the back of the mind distribute emptiness inside me, expose me totally.

There are memories for digging into words without defiling graves. Closeness is a rooting. I cannot get close to any you. No otherness, only an alternation in appearance. I need all my tensions and lightness. Albuquerque must not explode in my head.

Entering Albuquerque I feel tired, I am fit of laughter, twisted words, baroque head in reality's beauty of a game. Suddenly.

Grazie welcomed me warmly. She was tender, attentive and joyous, stroked the tattoo on my shoulder. Very sensuous. Then we ate, laughed, and I drank nonstop until sentences began between us to distribute playfulness, to enumerate memories, to share out time. Grazie loved to talk and I loved her perfume. She talked to me about wounds, about dancing, about a series of photographs taken in front of the mirror. I know not why but between every one of her sentences I thought of Lorna, of that way she has of making herself intelligible between two twisted sentences and my mother's soft arms.

'Grazie, come, it's cold in this big bed. Come. Go away. Turn the light on. Turn it off. I'm going to read all night. You should sleep. You see it's soft, touch me a bit, you see, wait … Just once, feels so good.'

Life goes off, life goes on. Tonight I will sleep, forlorn little animal, in the hollow of Grazie's incense-filled sleep.

4

O'blongman emerged from the night and recovered his body. It was still dark. No noise to ward off isolation. O'blongman raised himself up with difficulty as if the night had been one of much drinking. He leaned against the wall, noticed that his hat had rolled to the foot of the bed. *Tomorrow,* he thought, the sky will be beautiful. But everywhere still, daybreak in him was fragmented. The figures he had drawn on the walls came up to him, followed him step by step in the little room. O'blongman, who had devoted his life to hoping for beauty, understood that once encased in science beauty could only fade. He would not be able to sustain the forced rhythm of the equations either, his insatiable appetite for knowledge. He felt vulnerable and bitter. He closed his eyes and surrendered to the fitful voice imploring inside him, *libera, memento,* tomorrow the sky would be blue, there would be no more waste in the atmosphere.

Grazie and her mother have gone out to the mall. Here I am, behind the window, and I'm watching reality go by. Nothing. I see nothing. Only reality. Some day I will exit all this mess. Beauty is before reality.

For the moment, take to the desert road again, get back to the Motel, the pool, the swimsuit girls. Reality will appear topless under the lights while the hired killers follow their instructions to the letter. The mind is fragile. It isn't easy to substitute images, to ally the abyss and plenitude within oneself. Grazie will never be 15.

On the way back, I drove fast, *fata de fata*. Why daydream while imagining kisses, embraces, while thinking that light is beautiful among the *ocotillos* and *paloverdes*? They gleam, the motels, the trailers, the tin, the pylons, even the rust and all those tires like dried-up condoms. That's the desert. I bought a case of Coke and I'm drinking. I'm thirsty. Reality makes me thirst.

I was 15 and I was watching reality encroach on beauty to make it parade and parody, as if the hidden flaw of violence wanted to grope at everything. In the harsh light, humanity's trembling aura was defending itself against reality.

Reality was rushing by. From time to time humanity would crop up around trailers and snack-bars. It was a woman in a T-shirt, enlarged by a thousand pregnancies, children imprinted onto her fate. Reality was rushing by, skilfully skirting atavisms, chance, destiny like an electric current. It was now a body half-buried under the hood of a car. Now a pair of jeans, a hat, shadows pinned to the ground. It was alternation of fiction, of desert and of beauty. Expanses in the mind.

Episodes when approaching cities. Yes, I was attracted by reality, fascinated by its multiple facets, its prose torn between daily matter and desire's fussiness. But reality was operating without a mandate in the thinking body's volume. Actualizing easy paths, the *déjà*-thought of instinct, humiliating the passionate desire for splendor. I was but a desiring shape in the contour of the aura encircling humanity. I would have to come upon it unexpectedly, there, in its impossible dimension.

Yes, I needed a body to face the unthinkable, a body that could filter lies, violence, fear, at night like at dawn, a body capable of diverting lightning, of distancing the cry tenacious with instinct.

I was driving, perfect on the edge of solitude. Desiring only the horizon, a little light as is natural during the day, the smell of the desert.

But it was cold in the desert night and everywhere that heat gave life, I trembled that it would shift everything over onto the side of death. I was trembling with the fear of turning reality into an episode by getting close to beings.

5

O'blongman is taking his shower. He likes water, for water to caress and lull the torment on his skin. Then his whole body surrenders. He lifts his head and water penetrates through the mouth, the ears, the nostrils, limns long streaks on his bony body. O'blongman would have liked his body muscular. He would have liked to touch that new body, to stroke its chest, to feel the firm buttocks, the arms, to squeeze the hard thighs. He would have felt unburdened of the figures and his hunched back would have straightened up ready for any sparring match. O'blongman would have liked to wrestle man-to-man. The throbbing heart, the pumping veins, the effort of muscles straining would inevitably have intoxicated him and the sweat of the ordeal would have been unlike his perspiration during the hours spent doing figures. He would have loved every movement and so very much his opponents' body. O'blongman was not thinking about the explosion anymore. He was action, tension, contraction and all abandon in the arms of the one he would have liked to be. He got out of the shower, looked at himself in the mirror, saw his hollow cheeks. The beard. He dressed in a hurry. Outside day was about to break but o'blongman pretended as though nothing. The curtains were drawn. Only the light from the explosion shone upon his gestures. O'blongman did not see the envelope slipped under the door.

I was thinking about Angela Parkins. I could see her tense face, her threatening mouth, the aim of her words, in her eyes, humanity well-targeted. But what did Angela Parkins see when her gaze braved erosion? How did she shape her numbers, how did her gestures in the heat and thirst attest to love's rapture?

I would soon be back at the Motel. Evenings I would devote myself to fear in front of the television set. In the daytime, there would be girls in swimsuits, at night, conversations in the Bar. In the daytime, my mother would be like a woman. At night, Lorna would be with my mother and I would get crazy over their veiled presence. I would get behind the wheel again. All this time, my thoughts would be attracted elsewhere, precise and cold. All this time, I would be watching. In reality, I would in no way yield before the tragic aura. Some day I would experience everything in synchrony, ecstasy, the secrets which from within undermine dear civilization. Beauty was before reality and reality was in writing, a gaping.

6

Day was there, behind the curtains, but o'blongman was not yet ready to face the light. He lit a cigarette, took a book at random from among the ones lying on the dresser. A great calm. A pervasive calm which, as he felt it rise inside him, was immediately compensated by a mental excitation which painfully revived every nerve, made the skin too raw. He was breathing slowly but knew he was being performed by an uncontrollable force. O'blongman turned the volume down, spotted the white envelope, got up, parted the curtains, then seemed to sadden over the little blue morning, still blue like the porcelain of his childhood Sunday noons. On the Motel lawn, a woman was moving a garden hose. The glittering morning entered o'blongman's head. He leaned over and picked up the envelope.

I had been driving all night. I would soon be back in Tucson but I was not yet ready to face the panic fear and the repeating dailiness of the Mauve Motel.

I chose to stop at the Red Motel which was run by a friend of my mother's. I would make up a story, I would tell of my tiredness and my inability to keep driving. The manager would offer me a room. I would get my bag out of the car. From the glove compartment I would take the composition book, the revolver would be hot. Then I would take possession of *my* room. I would write all morning. The room would be small, commonplace, the curtain see-through, my body very calm in this anonymous setting. I would have the impression of understanding everything, night, Grazie, my mother, Lorna and all the other women living inside me. I would slip deeply into that intimate something which in reality rules everything. My hand would be slow. Humanity would be unable to repeat itself. I would be inventive. I would be watchful, sure-tongued, quick-witted.

7

O'blongman examines each photograph. No doubt about it, the explosion was successful. A photograph is striking evidence. Reality which was an ordeal in o'blongman's head is now an exposed shape on the photograph, fine print. O'blongman is free. 'It's nothing, it's nothing.' It's all in the photograph. O'blongman pins the prints to the wall as for a final scrutiny. He moves back, moves up. Looks at the explosion. He turns the light on, turns it off, closes the curtains, seeking the perfect lighting which could slick the scene: the gaze's finishing touch. Then the black and white of the photographs transform the whole room into a huge snapshot. O'blongman looks out the window. Outside all is color. The pool, the swimsuits, the parasols, the water. O'blongman lights a cigarette. The whole room is solarized.

Reality imposes itself around the pool. Here I am in my life of 15 years having become a character, pure adventure in theatrical time. The light is bright, slides over the tiles, decomposes rainbow in the gaze. Arms, thighs, backs, chests. Light assails the infinitely precious desire to live.

A young woman is taking pictures. Two others are posing. Music enters their smile, bursts of laughter bleached out by the light. Eyelids blink. The light is harsh. For a moment, eternity is beginning again. The sound of voices, murmurs, ad lib, the taste of cocktails under tongue. A man comes up to the posing women, starts a conversation in French. The man is thin. I can't hear what he is saying. The women laugh. He gets up, goes to the bar. The light is bright. He comes back with a glass of whiskey. He speaks with great courtesy between his sentences. He is not from here. He is not French either. I'm thirsty. I look toward the bar. A dive. The man goes by me again. He stretches his body out on a black and white striped towel. The light is harsh. Time wears thin. The girls chat while bobbing their legs in the water. I dive in. Reality is a desire spaced throughout memory. Motels are alike, reality, intrusive.

I will swim a little. A few lengths, mammal, cetacean, ranid, and then shower as the tourists leave for the desert to see orange erupting and feel mauve slowly moving them away from anxiety. When they get back, I will be at the bar and the manager will say as though this were reassuring that I now look like a woman. Then eyes fixed upon the mirror behind the bar, I will witness the procession of customers ordering multicolored drinks and seeking in the taste the calming effect of sunset.

8

O'blongman is reciting Sanskrit poems. The explosion is far away. The knot of his tie, well done. The photographs lie amid the equations. O'blongman feels light, almost happy. He is ready, at last, to meet the authorities. One last night at the motel, then he will regain his true identity, his confident charm. He knows how to argue and convince. He will be impeccable. O'blongman saw his awkward body in the mirror. 'It is snowing in the everlasting.' He put on his jacket and headed for the Bar.

It's Thursday evening. Customers are arriving in couples or one by one. The Bar is full of accents, some tourists, a few regulars make the rounds, parade around the bar. I know all of this.

No plot can hold up to the desert. The desert drinks everything in, anatomy, thoughts apparently capable of hope. One must be able to invent around one's 15 years. Be capable of everything. To dramatize, daring stunt over the horizon, to transform the cascading waters of little falls into light wells, immobilize the dark, in a single leap traverse all probabilities. Here in the Bar of the Red Motel, the desert is out of place. There remains only thirst unbridled like a torrent capable of sweeping away all bone structures, the dry core of the soul. I grew up in the desert. I have no merit in wanting it true. I grew up in solitude. I am protecting myself against the world's crappy aspect.

The man with the accent has just made his entrance. He nods to the poolside women. I order a beer. The owner whispers a few words which certainly make me a young woman. She greets all her people warmly. The music is playing full-blast. People are dancing, trying to match their steps, to fit together by arranging their bodies to the rhythm. Arms are raised in the shape of capes as if to capture the warm tan of faces. At the far end of the room, the skinny man is leaning against the wall and smoking.

Dawn orients energy. I need dawn. I want to understand everything. I'm thirsty. Somebody brushes against me. Angela Parkins moves all around me, joyous and cavalier. Time slows, her presence thrills me. The music explodes in my head. The 3 pool women have found partners. The skinny man is speaking with 2 other men. The music is beating loud. Bodies take off, horses at full gallop, manes lassoed by the lighting, blue eyes, blond faces, shadows on foreheads, the girls' flaring smiles, the color of suntanned gestures. Everything is sensuous. I look at Angela Parkins. She signals widely to me, comes toward me, takes me by the waist. The music is too loud. The music is still too soft. Angela Parkins' body capers about, crazy deer with eyes full of wildness. High-flying body, vertigo body. They are looking at us. They are watching us. Beauty suddenly, slyly. There is singing between Angela's lips, there is bawling, troating, chanting. Our hands meet, freeze, brushing skin's velvet smoothness, clasp each other in the low-throated whisper of words. It is like a great tournament of sound. Then her cheek at last close up.

I have known Angela Parkins for such a short time and yet here we are in a state of such closeness. But for eternity, there is no more space between us. We are the desert and *matter* of fact. In our eyes no more turmoil, only America sonorous and distant blending with the color of skins. Perhaps a bit more night. Dancing together the 3 women avoid getting too close. The music is too loud. Angela Parkins suggests we sit down. We are drinking the same thing. Then in my head the brouhaha stops and Angela is talking about existing. She is saying everything is going to begin again, speech, paths, feelings, she is saying that crying forces one to slow down, that in distress all sounds overcome the mouth, that they are raw material in the mouth, that it becomes difficult then to understand oneself, she is saying that things are blowing in her head and that if the world were to be attempted again, still more storms would be needed, electricity everywhere in the mind, she is saying that one must hope, that memory can still accomplish works of beauty, but the eyes, Mélanie, she is saying that in reality a few concise words are enough to change the course of death, to frighten away little pains, she is talking and awakening in me the horizon.

It is half past midnight. Night keeps finding its way through the music, making its nest between our legs. Time is working meticulously. Muscle, nerve, cell, vertigo skin organize in us mirages, visions.

One more time, more music, we're dancing gaily. Then Angela Parkins' body is moving so little. I tighten my grip on her waist. It's hot between us, against the temples, in the hair. Angela, we're dancing? No more echo, no more music. Our bodies no longer hold together. The silence is harsh. The eyes, quick the eyes! The pupil, desire's great work, is wilting. Chair noises, commotion, voices that carry. The devastation is great. O'blongman stares straight ahead, completely detached from the scene. Angela Parkins is stretched out on the blond wood of the dance floor, her body forever inflexible, displayed, point of viewing. Mélanie, daughter of the night, what happened?

Reality, dawn. Nothingness. My whole body is about to submit. Policemen, chalk around the corpse. Nobody saw a thing. I didn't see anything coming. The desert is indescribable. Eyes wilt.

Then came the threatening profile of every thing. Then dawn, the desert and mauve, the horizon. There are memories for digging into words without defiling graves. I cannot get close to any you.

Nicole Brossard was born in Montreal, Quebec, in 1943. Co-founder and editor of the reviews *la Barre du Jour* (1965) and *la Nouvelle Barre du Jour* (1977), she is the author of 19 collections of poetry, seven novels, a play, essays and several pieces for radio, and co-director of the film *Some American Feminists* (1986). Brossard is an active participant in international colloquia and conferences on literature and feminism. She has twice won the Governor General's Award for poetry in French, for *Mécanique jongleuse* (1975) and *Double Impression* (1984).

Susanne de Lotbinière-Harwood is a Montreal writer, translator and performative lecturer.

Editor for the Press: Frank Davey
Book Format: Nicole Brossard
Cover Design and Interior Graphics: Shari Spier / Reactor
Cover Illustration: Tom Hunt
Photographs: R.-Max Tremblay
Interior Illustration: Richard Misrach
Text Design: Nelson Adams
Typeset in Adobe Garamond
Printed in Canada

COACH HOUSE PRESS
401 (rear) Huron Street
Toronto, Canada M5S 2G5